Limbo Beirut

Emerging Voices from the Middle East

Series Editor
Tarek El-Ariss

Other titles in the series include *I Want to Get Married!*
and *A Bit of Air*.

Limbo Beirut

HILAL CHOUMAN

Translated by Anna Ziajka Stanton

CENTER FOR MIDDLE EASTERN STUDIES

THE UNIVERSITY OF TEXAS AT AUSTIN

Cover image: Cover illustrations © Fadi Adleh. Courtesy of the artist.

Library of Congress Control Number: 2016933841
ISBN: 978-1-4773-1005-2

INTERIOR ILLUSTRATIONS:
Illustrations in Chapter 1 by Fadi Adleh. © Fadi Adleh.
Courtesy of the artist. fadiadleh.deviantart.com.

Illustrations in Chapter 2 by Barrack Rima. © Barrack Rima.
Courtesy of the artist. barrackrimaa.blogspot.com.

Introductory illustration and illustrations in Chapter 3 by Jana Traboulsi.
© Jana Traboulsi. Courtesy of the artist. ayloul.blogspot.com.

Illustrations in Chapters 4 and 5 by Mohamed Gaber. © Mohamed Gaber.
Courtesy of the artist. portfolio.gaberism.net.

Originally published in Arabic in 2013 as Līmbū Bayrūt by Dar al-Tanweer.
Dar al-Tanweer granted permission for the creation of this English translation.

This book was funded in part by a generous grant from the Shaibani Donor Fund.

To all those whose smiles met mine in friendship, yet beyond this they remained strangers to me. To the faces I passed by chance more than once on the streets of Beirut, and which stayed with me although I did not actually know their owners. To those who carry stories with them and do not tell them to anyone.

—HILAL CHOUMAN

Translator's Note

Limbo Beirut is the third novel by Lebanese writer Hilal Chouman
(b. 1982). In spare prose that is at times deceptively simple, at
times luminously poetic, Chouman weaves together diverse
narrative strands into a polyvocal portrait of life in twenty-first-
century Beirut. The backdrop for the novel's principal events
is the clashes between Hezbollah militants and fighters loyal
to the Future Movement that rocked the Lebanese capital in
May 2008—a conflict that received little coverage in the Western
media but which shook the country deeply and inspired fears
that the sectarian divisions that embroiled Lebanon in a brutal
civil war from 1975 to 1990 would once again send it spiraling
into violence. The significance for modern Lebanese society
of the civil war, which devastated central Beirut and killed an
estimated 120,000 people while displacing some one million
more, cannot be overstated. The psychological scars left by the
war are still fresh for many Lebanese who lived through it,
and it has been a dominant theme in the country's literature,
cinema, and art over the past four decades.

With the passage of time, however, the war has gradually begun to recede into the past. Under a massive and controversial initiative backed by the government of the late billionaire prime minister Rafik Hariri, some areas of the heavily damaged old downtown have been restored while others were cleared and rebuilt with modern high-rises, restaurants, and a shopping mall mimicking a traditional Arab bazaar. For a broad segment of Lebanese youth today who were too young to have fought in the war themselves, the traumas that defined a previous generation can be felt and experienced only at a distance. All of the characters in Limbo Beirut remember the civil war, but with the exception of one, they were children during its worst years. Their recollections of it are fragmentary, disjointed, condensed into a memory of hiding behind window shutters that remained permanently closed for security or of hours spent solving crossword puzzles when it was too dangerous to go outside. The events of May 2008—with sectarian militias assembling in the streets, the sound of gunfire in the city center, and the glow of rocket-propelled grenades illuminating the night sky—summon these long-buried memories abruptly and painfully to the surface. Yet frightening though the violence is, it also functions to push these young men and women beyond the banalities of their everyday lives. One character steals paint from his boyfriend's house and covers a neighborhood wall in surrealist graffiti. Another composes hundreds of feverish pages of the novel he has been trying to write for years. Another gives birth. In Limbo Beirut's final chapter, as tensions ease and the city slowly returns to normal, a young doctor is finally able to move on from his failed romantic relationship and begin to build new connections with his fellow citizens of the capital and with Beirut itself.

Released under the Arabic title Līmbū Bayrūt in 2013 by publisher Dar al-Tanweer, Chouman's novel is a boldly modernist, even postmodern, text. Its five chapters, in which we witness the same scenes play out from multiple angles as our viewpoint rotates cinematically among the novel's two female and five male narrators, could theoretically be read in any order—although I suggest that there is, at the same time, a profound logic to the sequence in which Chouman has placed them that should not be disregarded. In a reminder of literature's unrivaled ability to both enrich and unsettle our sense of perspective, characters whose minds we inhabit in one chapter reappear elsewhere as secondary actors, so that we see them also as they are perceived by others and not only as they see themselves. Each chapter contains some fifteen black-and-white drawings done expressly for the book by various contemporary Arab artists. These illustrations, which range from the fanciful to the frankly disturbing, offer striking visual renditions of some of the narrative's main events. Yet rather than limiting our ability to imagine these scenes for ourselves, the illustrations are provocative; they invite us to engage with the text on all levels and with all senses firing.

Perhaps it is the sensory participation that the text demands of us that made translating Limbo Beirut an experience at once personally affecting and disorienting. A certain suspension of one's own place and history, one's filtered and narrow lens on the world, is a prerequisite to translating literature. Only by setting these things aside can a translator become capable of transmitting words composed by another person in a foreign idiom into her own language honestly and ethically, capturing their particularity, their difference, and their beauty. Yet to translate also means engaging with the text in an extraordinarily intimate manner that leaves no part of the translator uninvolved or untouched. This is the same paradox we all face as readers of translated literature: How can we suspend our disbelief, leave our biases and preconceptions behind, and lose ourselves in what may seem at first a wholly alien world, while never renouncing or forgetting the humanity we share with all people near and far? There is no perfect answer to this question, but while reading *Limbo Beirut* it is one I urge all of us to keep in mind.

Anna Ziajka Stanton
January 2016

Limbo Beirut

I

The Little Prince

ILLUS. FADI ADLEH

HE COULDN'T SLEEP. Yet he stayed in bed. He fixed his gaze on the clothes cupboard against one wall. Its door, he saw, stood slightly ajar. Beyond it was a narrow hallway, bounded by the door's shadow on the wood floor in collaboration with the light in the corridor. Was it the bed, to which he had not yet grown accustomed? Or the May heat? He could not identify an obvious cause for his insomnia. He curled up like a fetus in his mother's belly and tried not to move. He hugged himself. He closed himself in upon himself. Knees secured against chest, doubled so that his feet nearly touched his buttocks. His hands gathered up his legs, folded in his knees, closer and closer.

When this state comes upon him, sleep abandons him and he is left with a peculiarly empty feeling. This time, he tried counting sheep so he would fall asleep faster. That had been Alfred's advice. He had told him: "Look up at the ceiling and start counting, and I bet you'll be asleep after the twenty-fifth sheep."

Walid counted. He got past twenty-five. He counted many sheep, yet he could not fall asleep. At first he counted with his eyes, yet soon he tired of staring at the blank ceiling. He began to fill it in with his imagination but found that this was even more exhausting.

Suddenly everything began to expand. His head swelled; his thoughts proliferated until they lost all semblance of order. The creatures he had drawn on the ceiling became irritable (his mother's habitual irritability before his father's death), hateful (his hatred of spinach and rice), stupid (like the politician from his neighborhood), commercial (repugnant commercialism, not the kind that inspires artistic ideas).

He decided to erase everything and restore to the ceiling the emptiness that was in his head, this emptiness that he was, now, beginning to lose.

And so the memories took over.

★ ★ ★

Walid rolled over and found Alfred sleeping on the other side of the bed. His mouth open, deep in slumber, he clutched the edge of his pillow in his hands like a child who fears the loss of his favorite toy. Walid noticed that Alfred had put on weight compared to how he'd been when they first met. He looked at the small blemish on the part of his hip closest to his back, and the tattoo on the joint of his foot, and the lip of his protruding paunch. In his sleep Alfred looked like any other man in his late thirties who returns from work every evening exhausted, plays with his child half asleep, and then joins his wife in bed. The image assailed Walid. Was it possible for Alfred to start a family? Was it possible for he himself to start a family?

The idea seemed some variety of impossible.

When Alfred had asked him to move in with him, Walid had refused. He explained that he did not have "relationships." *Let's remain as we are. We meet up, we forget the troubles of the day, we enjoy ourselves and then we sleep. If we lived together, we would suffocate each other. We would bring all our outside worries into the house.* "Let's keep it like this," Walid said. *Let's stay strangers. Shy every time we meet. Enthralled by each minute we spend on superficial questions about the period we were apart.* "Let's keep it like this," he said. *I come from my apartment in the Caracas neighborhood to your place on Rue Clemenceau whenever we want to see each other.*

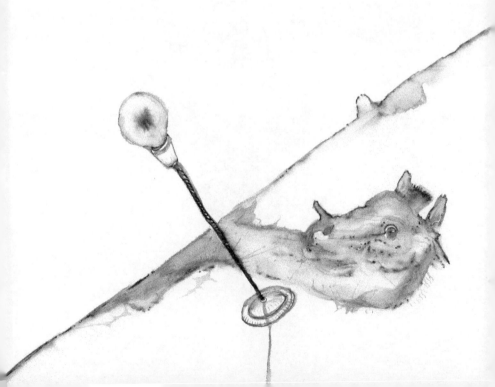

Alfred did not argue with him. He was silent. Then he said, "As you like." Walid was sure that Alfred would repeat his request soon, and he reflected upon the extent of time during which his *No* would have to hold its ground. He never imagined that the matter would be settled so quickly: he was there for a visit, and he got stuck.

He didn't know whether he could describe his coming to Clemenceau as a *visit*. He didn't know whether it was really *getting stuck*. The latter was Alfred's turn of phrase. He had said it to him, and it had adhered peculiarly in his mind.

When the first clashes broke out, he was with Alfred on the balcony. He couldn't remember what time it was. Maybe five o'clock in the evening, or just before, or a little after. Press conferences were held, breaking news headlines ran at the bottom of every screen (though Walid and Alfred did not read them). They imagined many raised fingers pointing at the sky (though they did not see them), and they expected more than furrowed brows, more than sweat on a few foreheads. What reached their ears was shouting . . . a lot of shouting.

On the balcony, Walid thought how unpleasant that sound was on a calm night like this.

The apartments in the neighboring buildings lit up, one after another. Suddenly there was no more power rationing. Suddenly the electricity of Lebanon was bestowed upon all.

From the balcony, Walid and Alfred nodded at men in their fifties who had left their televisions on inside and come out to see what was happening. All of them were smoking, above each a protective cloud forming. Their wives stayed indoors. Probably they were following the news, Walid thought.

Only moments later, crimson shots tore through the sky.

Gentle showers of bullets became audible, their low pitch betraying that they came from interior Beirut and not from the coast. The scene reminded Walid of one from E.T., the film dearest to his heart. Standing in the middle of the frame, E.T. indicates something with his facial expressions that the other actors do not understand. Then, in the next shot, he appears pointing his finger straight up and saying, "Home."

Had these men in their fifties, now pointing their fingers at the rain of bullets, seen this all before? Were they reclaiming old customs? Did they remember how they used to go out onto the rooftops as teenagers and wait for the evening round of shelling?

As the men continued smoking and talked among themselves from balcony to balcony and from roof to roof, Walid imagined that they were happy, the lot of them, extraordinarily happy.

What now?

And so the memories took over.

★ ★ ★

Walid sat up in bed, lowered his left leg to the ground, and began to study the room. The wooden floor struck him as bourgeois, he who had come from a middle-class family that did not see the need for anything but simple patterned tiles, or in rare circumstances inexpensive marble flagstones, and then only in the living room and family room. He remembered as a child seeing the wooden floors in a friend's apartment and suggesting that very day to his father, who was making plans to renovate and paint their apartment, that together they could install wood flooring at least in the bedrooms.

His mother had intervened, objecting, "What for? So we can stuff the dirt and filth underneath it?" She had already prepared her counterargument: she told them about the family of mice that their neighbors had found under the wooden floor they'd installed in their apartment—and of course they regretted it now, she said.

Walid realized then that he had lost his silly battle. One glance at his father's face told him that it was his mother who decided these matters. His father met his look with a smile, and then both of them laughed. In an instant they became allies in the face of his mother's arguments, though she was quick to respond with a new preemptive attack: "Go on, laugh. Your laughter won't change anything!"

The wooden floor in Alfred's room was an exact replica of the one he had seen in his friend's apartment. In spite of the years that had passed, his memory had retained the color of the wood. He knew that were he to get up and open Alfred's laptop, he would be able to find it in Adobe InDesign with remarkable ease, despite the many color gradations present to choose from.

Alfred's laptop sat on a long wooden table, broad and bare of designs, that extended from the right-hand corner of the room to a supporting column on the left side. Behind the desk, a plate glass window of matching length prevented the construction of shelves. On the two ends of the table, scraps of paper and books, pens, a camera and lenses, and many other odds and ends were collected. Apart from these mountains on its margins, the rest of the desk was empty except for the laptop and the cord connecting it to the electrical outlet.

Walid lowered his other leg from the bed and stood up carefully. His bare feet touched the wood. He went over to his shoes and his clothing, which was thrown across a chair next to the open clothes cupboard. He tried to tie the drawstring on the front of the voluminous shorts that Alfred had given him so that they wouldn't fall down, and then he began to move slowly through the room, taking care not to step on the piles of clothes and plastic bags strewn in the way. The empty middle portion of the desk seemed out of place beside the papers massed on its ends and the chaos on the floor, or the cupboard with its guts spilling out.

The next time Alfred asked him to move in with him, Walid's retort had been, "You're messy." Alfred looked at him in surprise, so he continued, "I'm serious. You're really messy. And I'm obsessively organized. It won't work out."

Alfred just laughed and said, "Fine, fine," and that day Walid laughed along with him, but he wasn't comfortable

with the way Alfred had accepted his answer. He laughed only because he wanted to bring their conversation about the move to an end.

Before he reached the other side of the bed where Alfred was sleeping, Walid's eyes were drawn to the pictures taped to the wall. He approached them slowly. As he studied them, he ran his hands over the sparse books on the shelf beside them. He paid no attention to two black-and-white photos of himself that Alfred had put up a few days ago. He was looking intently at his favorite poster.

The poster showed Nadia Lutfi, Hind Rostom, and Shadia all together. Alfred had taken poses of the three actresses from their most famous films and made the women appear to be in one place. They looked as if they were interconnected in some way, even though each of them was doing something different. When Walid had declared that Shadia was an outsider to the Nadia/Hind pair, Alfred replied, "It's none of your business," and laughed.

Walid's fingers continued unconsciously caressing the meager books. The books tipped slightly but did not fall. He was fascinated by the poster. Suddenly it became clear to him that Shadia was not in the least an outsider. He discovered a detail that he couldn't quite quantify. The three actresses now seemed like squabbling sisters who had stepped out of a story in *A Thousand and One Nights*, yet at the same time they appeared to a great extent in harmony with one another. For a moment he wondered whether they had indeed all acted together in a single film — although he never watched Arabic films.

Walid turned around, looking at Alfred. He had not been able to see this side of him from his previous position in the bed.

أُفيش

أُفيش

أُفيش

أُفيش

Once again he could see only his face, the upper half to be exact, from his forehead to the tip of his nose. The lower half of his face was missing, hidden under the edge of the pillow he held.

In his drawings, Walid focused on precisely that part of the face. He devoted special care to it, worked for hours refining it. One time, he had begun by drawing the upper half of a face, and before it was complete he moved on to drawing the upper half of another face on the same sheet of paper. After two hours, he stepped back and surveyed what he had drawn. He found dozens of half-faces. All of them were without chins or mouths.

Alfred had seen the half-faces and observed sarcastically, like a teenager who hasn't forgotten a comment that annoyed him, "I'm messy and you're obsessively organized?"

Walid paid no attention to Alfred and went back to drawing. Without mouths the faces spoke to Walid, and he knew from their upper halves the nature of the lower halves that he must create. The first indicated the second. Working without interruption, he completed the drawing on the following day. Everything had been planned out in his head, and when the drawing was finished, it was as if it had been done in a single sitting.

When Alfred saw it again, he smiled. He said nothing, but his silence did not conceal his admiration. On a later visit, Walid arrived to find him photographing the drawing. He asked Walid's permission with a tilt of his head, and Walid for his part gestured to him that he was welcome to continue. He kept taking photos for a few more minutes, and then he showed them to Walid. Finally he erased them all, keeping only one. As he looked at the photos on the screen, he did not stop smiling.

The same smile was on Alfred's face now as he slept. Walid could identify it by the number of creases in his forehead.

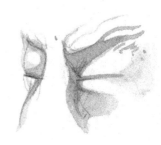

As if he were dreaming with great concentration.

Alfred shifted in the bed. The pillow he had been hugging fell to the ground.

His naked chest appeared, and with it the Japanese tattoo. When Alfred had taken off his shirt for the first time in Walid's presence, Walid had been startled by the tattoo. It was one of the few times he had seen a tattoo in just this spot, over the left nipple. Over the heart. He asked about the language of the tattoo, and Alfred answered, "Japanese." He asked him about its meaning, and Alfred told him, "Later."

When, later, Walid repeated his question, Alfred countered, "What do you think?"

"I never guess anything right."

"Try, maybe you'll get it this time."

Walid raised the left corner of his lips slightly, his cheek rounding, in an involuntary expression that he often made when embarrassed. Alfred insisted again that he should guess.

"Your name?"

"No."

"*Peace?*" he offered in English.

"Nope."

"*Love?*"

(Alfred took a drag on his cigarette and raised his eyebrows in a No.)

Walid felt his own ineptitude keenly each time he gave a wrong answer. Eventually he stopped guessing. He had used up his attempts. He seized the pack of cigarettes from the bed nervously, opened it, and withdrew a cigarette.

Alfred laughed and said, "You don't like to lose."

"Wrong. I always lose," he replied, lighting his cigarette.

After this exchange, Walid waited for Alfred to explain the meaning of the tattoo to him, but he didn't. He became occupied with something else, and Walid never remembered to ask him again during their subsequent meetings.

But of course, he did remember. He only avoided asking, and Alfred didn't bring up the topic again.

In spite of this, Walid carried out his research as best he could. He memorized the image. It didn't take more than a few glances, only for a few seconds each time, while Alfred was sleeping or not paying attention. The Internet made his task easier. He went to Japanese websites. He submersed himself in the alien shapes until he found the object of his search: the repeated shape that comprised the tattoo.

He copied and pasted it, twice in a row, into Google Translate:

ここ

It gave him the answer in English:

Here

And in Arabic:

هُنا

Now Walid grabbed cardstock, pens, and scissors from the materials at the ends of the desk. He sat cross-legged on the floor and began to copy the tattoo. He could have drawn it without looking. But he wanted to do it the old-fashioned way to avoid mistakes.

Sometimes particular details caught his attention, became by themselves enough to remind him of an entire scene or object. When he told Alfred about this talent, Alfred greeted it with indifference: "Of course. That's your visual memory." As usual, Walid regretted disclosing his secret. His powers of speech were diminishing bit by bit with the passage of time, and he began to feel anew that his foolishness was growing ever greater, accumulating. So he decided that he would not talk at all except in times of urgent need, that he would become a creature of utter silence.

But as always when he made such decisions, Walid let this one drop. There was something about being with Alfred that made him abandon his resolve at the least pretext. This time, he told himself that perhaps he had misidentified the problem.

In the bed, Alfred smiled. If Walid hadn't been certain that he was asleep, he would have said that Alfred knew what he was doing, and that he was watching him. Alfred never stopped laughing. His laughter was vulgar in its quantity, whereas his smile was less frequent, indeed almost rare. Walid had another theory that had been proven correct as the days passed: Alfred didn't mean anything by his laughter, but he certainly meant something by his smiles.

On the balcony, with the men in their fifties nearby, Alfred had laughed as usual and said to Walid, "The war has started, baby." He took a drag on a hash cigarette and passed it to him. Walid refused and gave it back, saying that he had no desire to smoke today.

Still laughing, Alfred observed, "Usually when a war starts, the hash becomes plentiful. Good varieties, not dry or anything. We'll even get the oil, I swear to God. The oil!"

Walid greeted the laughter sharply. "You're dreaming! War? This is all no big deal. It's nothing to get excited about. Everything that can happen has already happened to this country. Everything that can be done was done before."

"But that doesn't mean it can't be done again!"

When did this happen? Three days ago? Four? Five? The days ran together for Walid when he drew. When he was inside the thing, isolated from everything except certain exterior details that alone, he did not know how, pierced his bubble. When he was inside the chaos trying to create order.

But could he really organize the chaos, could he set it right? Or was he only adding it to the chaos already inside him: chaos amplified by chaos.

Since yesterday, it had been within his power to return to Caracas. He didn't "get stuck," as Alfred had said. The distance between the Clemenceau and Caracas areas was not great, and he could walk via Hamra, where no battles of note were happening. The main battle, whose bullets they had been hearing in Clemenceau, was taking place at the axis of Mulla/Karakol El Druze–Hay El Lija/Zokak El Blat.

When he went out for a coffee on the second day of the clashes, Walid found the people in Hamra going on with their lives just as they did on regular days. Some men carrying weapons passed near him in a small truck piled high with foam mattresses. They were dressed in dark green and brown.

Walid knew from the look of the men and the load of mattresses that the fight would last longer than a day. Other than that, life on the street carried on, if modestly. There were not the customary crowds, and some of the newspapers belonging to certain political parties had disappeared from the news kiosks, but the few people who were out were behaving in an almost natural manner.

Walid noticed from the snatches of conversation he picked up that people were avoiding talk of what had happened. There was no sense of opposition among the men on the street. The owners of some of the stores that were open were even greeting the militants by name, and this made him ask: When did they have time to make friends with them?

Only the voices of the women resounded in protest against the harassment from some of the militants. Walid himself witnessed two altercations during his brief walk. In the first, a girl in her twenties stopped to curse the men and then went on her way. In the second, a woman in her forties (she looked like a journalist) practically attacked one of the men. In both cases, the men laughed and the women departed still cursing them.

Walid followed the two disputes from afar without interfering, as he stood sipping his coffee at a small shop on a side street. Making no attempt to engage Walid in conversation, the shop's proprietor remarked as though to himself, "These women are worth a hundred of us men."

It was with the same two words, *us men*, that Walid's father would begin his arguments with his mother when she tried to lure him into a quarrel. *Us men have no time for your foolishness. Us men have no time for these details, we're concerned with more important things. Us men wear ourselves out for the sake of . . .* Benign disagreements would be transformed between his parents into universal battles between all men and women, burdened with more significance than they could bear.

"It's all because of those shows you watch," his father would say, blaming their arguments on the morning television programs to which his wife devoted herself for long periods while she cooked.

And it was with the same two words, *us men*, that his father would begin the edifying lectures that he was bent on delivering to his son during his final days. Walid, even though inside he hated the lectures, felt an obligation to listen. In their interactions, his father had always treated him with a certain dignity and respect. He could not remember a single instance when they had fought, nor a single time when his father had hit him or shouted at him, even when he was a child. His mother took care of all these things, and he had turned to his father always as a refuge.

Perhaps for these reasons, and for other reasons as well, he had never for a day considered telling his father about his sexuality. Such a thing seemed impossible to him. The words *us men* could not be made to encompass news like this, however kind his father had always been to him.

Just when his mother began to ask him why he was not married, death took his father, and she had no time to cluck and fuss like other mothers. Walid expected her now to direct her quarrels at him, but a deep sadness enveloped her. She would not shed her black clothes, and she nearly stopped talking. Sometimes she remained silent for more than a day at a stretch. It had never occurred to him that his parents had loved each other. After his father's death, he reexamined many of his prior ideas about them. He took to poring over old photo albums. He read letters his father had written to his mother when they were young. He read them without his mother's knowledge, although she wouldn't have cared anyway, as she had begun to spend her days sleeping. Walid didn't understand at first. His mother, the devotee of morning TV programs and creator of arguments out of nothing, used to read love letters? His very uncomplicated mother—to her, once, love letters were written? It seemed to defy logic, but the picture became clearer as he delved into the letters and postcards.

POSTCARD

My sweet darling,
Time passes slowly when I'm far away from you.
Next month I'll be in Beirut.
Kuwait, 11 February 1977

Walid loved his mother afresh. He yearned to hear her scoff at his studies or his job as she once had. When she had protested to his father after he chose his university major—"What does he mean, *drawing*? He's a smart kid, never caused us any trouble when he was in school! Why drawing? Let him take up engineering!"—his father opposed her.

"The boy knows what he wants," he said. Once they were alone together, his father asked him, confirming that this was his choice, "You want this, *baba*?"

"Yes, Papa."

"Very well."

His mother cut him off for days. She never asked him anymore whether he wanted to eat. The sharpness of her ridicule increased. His father would laugh, and begin his sentences with *us men*, and they would chuckle together. After a time, they met alone in a Beirut café. And in one of his edifying lectures, his father said to him, "Don't be upset with your mother, *baba*. This is her way of communicating. Just ask me. But there's no one with a better heart."

His mother didn't change her behavior until Walid fell seriously ill. He was spending long nights at the university. He had become accustomed to consuming only coffee and cigarettes. He lost weight. He was unable to eat. He only drank liquids, and he burped all the time. He checked into the hospital for an endoscopy. His mother accompanied him. The doctor said, after he came out of the procedure, "No coffee, and he needs to watch what he eats and when he eats it." He explained, as he wrote a prescription for the medicine Walid had to take, that a combination of psychological stress and irritation of the gastric membrane had produced an ulcer, and that it was possible the condition would get worse if Walid didn't follow his instructions.

His mother took charge of his new dietary regimen. She began to prepare each day's meals for him in small plastic containers, and she trailed him on his cell phone when he was out of the house. Sometimes she burst into his room asking if he had taken his medicine or demanding to know why he hadn't eaten his meal.

She used to communicate with him in her own way. Then she lost everything with the death of his father, and Walid lost her along with him. Though politics had become her chief preoccupation before her husband's death, she no longer watched TV or newscasts. They said that the government was fighting itself, that the country hated itself, that the explosion was inevitably coming. Walid's mother displayed no reaction to any of this news. The depth of her silence said that these things were incidental, that these news items were insignificant details and that which was of greatest importance in her life was her story with her dead husband. She turned her back on everything. Even on her son and his dietary regimen. For the first time Walid entered the kitchen. For the first time he felt like he was a bachelor. She stayed in her room, and he began to prepare food for her.

On the fourth of May, he went into her room. She was in bed. He shook her but she didn't respond. He thought she was sleeping. He brought a wooden chair and sat beside her. He stayed there contemplating her for an hour. She didn't wake up. It appeared to him as though her jaw had fallen off. That she had become half-faced, like his drawings. He brought a bandage and wrapped her face, closing her mouth. Then he picked up his cell phone and called the few members of the family who remained in the country to tell them of her death. They buried her the next day in El Bashoura cemetery. They buried her on top of his father. Walid stood over the grave that had opened twice in six months. This was the second time he was required to take up a shovel and scatter dirt upon a dead body in a bag. He did what was needed without hesitating as he had the previous time, the day his father died. He had become an expert.

Afterward, he stood shaking hands with many people he didn't know. Some kissed him, some hugged him, and some simply offered condolences. On the third day of the mourning period, he called Alfred and told him what had happened. Alfred came to his apartment. His manner was strained, and Walid had little to say. They sat in the living room for ten minutes, neither of them speaking a word, and then, apologizing, Alfred left. After half an hour, Walid picked up his cell phone and called him again. He asked him if he was busy, and Alfred replied that he was at home. An hour later, Walid found himself on the balcony of Alfred's apartment, crying in his lap.

Now, as he was finishing his drawing, everything inside of him seemed to turn over at the same instant, becoming without flavor or taste. His father's death. Sleeping in Alfred's bed. The hard wooden floor. The poster of the actresses. And this small war, so very well organized, so very limited, so very local.

Were it not for the fact that the comparison might be unlucky, he would have said that this war resembled his brain. He hadn't lived through the Lebanese Civil War in its entirety.

He could recall the end of it, the last two years to be exact. He remembered missing school a lot, and he remembered exploring East Beirut, breathless on the heels of his teenage friends. He remembered Sin El Fil, and Kaslik, and Jubail, and Jounieh. A few months after the public announcement that the war had ended, and with a single government having assumed power, his father took him to see downtown Beirut. He made him walk on top of the rubble. The chaos was staggering. There were many visitors, and when he and his father moved a short distance away his mother shouted at them to stay close. "No one knows, maybe there are still mines!"

His father took many photos of him. He had them photographed together. The whole family was photographed. Walid had saved the photos. These few photos were the access point. They were his "visual memory" of that visit, which he could recall in perfect detail. Since that day, he had known that he would draw. Since the moment he looked out over downtown Beirut, with its hummocks of dirt and its debris and its desolation, to find that it resembled hair, thick and disheveled. He could remember how it appeared to him from atop the mound of rubble he stood on. The image had visited him more than once in his dreams. Now, as he finished his drawing, he noticed what might seem normal, trivial to many: there was hair on the upper halves of the faces as well.

Walid rose, leaving what he had produced on the floor. He picked up the things he had borrowed—tools and paints and pens and scissors and knives—and he returned them all to their places at the desk's two ends. He stood for a moment, leaning with both hands on the lip of the desk. The morning

was verging on dawn. He saw a slender ray of light emerge from behind a cloud, and at just that moment the digital clock on the desk showed the time as five a.m. He was sweating. He turned around, giving his back to the sun as if he wanted the morning light to wipe the sweat from its cold surface. With his palm he brushed stray droplets from his forehead. Alfred was visible to him again. He had not moved. Only his facial expression had changed. Perhaps he has completed his dream, thought Walid. Perhaps he has completed his dream.

As if it were calling out to him, a small book fell from among the few on the shelf near the posters on the wall. Walid went over to straighten it, and when he saw its title he smiled. He looked again at Alfred, who was rolling over onto the other side of the bed, still asleep. He went to the chair, finished dressing in a hurry, and put on his shoes. He opened his bag, carefully stowed inside it what he had finished making on the floor earlier, put in the book as well, hurriedly added a few other items gathered from the top of the desk, and went out.

He walked through the streets alone. He observed that there were no cars passing. No cats on the trash bins. No garbage collectors in green suits on the corners. No people sipping an early coffee. Not one among the stores was open. The rays of light were increasing and widening shyly like they always did during the climactic scenes in the old Egyptian movies that Walid never watched. All that was needed now was musical accompaniment for every detail to finally cohere, and the hero to have his moment, and the chaos of the mind to be wiped clean. The music would hasten the passage of time, and trim the moment of everything extraneous, and later Alfred would honor the scene with another poster on the wall of his room.

Walid walked aimlessly until he found himself on Hamra Street. He stopped in front of a wall. He took his supplies out of the bag. First he tried to clean the wall, and then he began to cover it with the images he had created on the floor of Alfred's apartment. He struggled to make the stiff papers stick. Each time he put one up, it fell down. A young man walking his dog passed nearby. He tied the dog to a telephone pole and began to watch Walid, and then presently he approached to take over the task of attaching the papers. They did not exchange words. Walid only smiled at him and busied himself removing other supplies from the bag. Then he began to spray the wall with paint, taking care not to stain the young man's hands and clothing. He repeated the process several times, and then he stepped back and fixed his gaze upon the graffiti.

Looking at the wall, Walid thought of the book that Alfred's bookshelf had spit out and which he had tucked into his bag: The Little Prince, by Antoine de Saint-Exupéry.

He wanted to go to the bag and put away his things, which were scattered on the ground. He would have done so, but just then the young man untied his dog in a hurry and fled toward a side street. Walid did not understand what had happened. He turned to find a gun trained on him. The man holding the gun asked him what he was doing there, so near to the party headquarters. Walid remained silent and did not answer. His thoughts returned unbidden to the book ejected by the bookshelf. He wondered about the fate of the Little Prince at the end of the story, and he discovered that he did not remember the ending, not at all.

2 *Limbo*

ILLUS. BARRACK RIMA

I STOOD ALONE in the room with glass walls, in our house on a hill in Mansourieh, looking at Beirut shimmering in the distance. From my vantage point the capital seemed like the end of the world. If I tried to get in my car and go there, I thought, I would find land terminating in a great valley. This notion made a particular idea take root in my head and stick there like a song from the radio: Beirut is a deep valley, yet most of the time we hardly notice. We can spend our lives there, we can go down into it every day—but the moment we realize that we're living in a valley, we no longer know how to get there. We are above it, standing on the edge. It's wholly below us, wholly remote.

The lights on the hills between me and that deep valley started to flicker on and off, as though each hill were greeting another. The electricity rationing would commence in one neighborhood and end in the next. Then the lights would begin to tremble, flee the first hill, and settle swiftly upon the hill beside it. As if some button-pusher at the state power utility kept making mistakes and switching on each neighborhood only to immediately switch it off again. Before me, the wave of light marched across the hills until it reached my room.

The electricity went out.

Flipping a single switch was all it took to turn on the generator. The route from the room with glass walls to the electric box in the front hall included a few steps up and a few down. Takara had designed it. She had convinced me that the identity of each room had to be fundamentally different from every other one, and that these differences would be reflected in our living experience. She thought that a warm color for the walls suited the living room, and she selected a pale, sleepy color for the bedrooms and a vivid one for the office, appropriate for my work environment (so she said). Her renovations were not limited to colors but extended to a concern for the ceilings as well. Different ceiling heights make you feel like you're in more than a single place as you move around, she said. Here, the wooden floor is nearer to the ceiling, almost enclosing you. There, the engraved tiles together with the glass ceiling give you a sense of the room's capaciousness.

"This is a place for all our moods," she said.

When we began the project of moving into the house, she begged me to give her a month to work on it. She rented me a hotel room in Achrafieh and made sure I didn't come near her work area. She ordered me to focus on my novel. "I call you if I want something, you call me if you want reassurance. Do not worry, I will call. I will need money. Do not worry."

I was definitely not worried about her. I had no idea how she

managed to communicate with strange men whose language she didn't speak. How she explained her ideas to them and made them understand. Takara was always like this. She bore everything upon her own two shoulders, even in the most challenging circumstances. She planned projects from A to Z. When we were getting ready to go on vacation, she would take charge of all the necessary preparations. She read everything about the country in two languages and took notes. She decided on our schedule of activities, made reservations with airlines, booked local transportation and hotels. Not one detail was left unattended to, unresearched.

After we had taken several vacations together, I could no longer describe our vacations as vacations. I began to joke with her, "Isn't it time for you to work on one of your own projects?"

She never laughed, but she never got annoyed at my jokes either. On the contrary, she would bring out her laptop, pull up a map, and begin to concentrate, and though she remained silent, her face clearly asked: Where should we go?

This was our third year of marriage, and she still didn't understand my humor, making me almost certain that the spirit of humor must differ in some essential way from one culture to another. But the good thing was that my wisecracks never evolved into a misunderstanding with her.

I had met Takara when I was studying comparative literature at Goldsmiths College in London. I saw a young woman with black hair and narrow eyes sitting on the grass surrounded by books. After that we ran into each other often on the university campus. I would greet her and she would nod her head at me. Then I would go on with my reading, or she would continue her work. We didn't actually speak until the day we met by chance in Greenwich Park, in southeast London. I remember that it was a Sunday, and that the sun was shining with unaccustomed radiance for that time of year, and that the grass was greener than usual. Everything was primed for an interaction going beyond a nod and a hello.

We spent the afternoon hours roaming the streets of London. We got on buses and got off them. We ate sandwiches and treated ourselves to *feteer*. By six o'clock we had arrived in the south of London. It wasn't more than a week before our visits to each other's residences began to multiply. I would go to the women's dorm, and she would come to the apartment that I shared with some Moroccan friends.

After a month, she announced her desire to move out of the dorm. I said that I would look for an apartment for her. When I conveyed the news to my Moroccan friend Ghali, he berated me for being stupid. "*Hmar!* You idiot!" He explained that "the girl" was sending me a signal that she wanted us to move in together, and that I had to propose this to her.

Takara didn't agree immediately. She seemed displeased. Yet she returned with an affirmative answer two days later—two days I spent swearing to Ghali that I would kill him if things went wrong. He only laughed and said, "Everything's mizyan, my friend, it's fine."

Ghali was right, and the plan proceeded faster than I expected.

I lived with Takara for a year. We carried out our life like a married couple. We learned when to be quiet and when to talk. When we were enjoying our personal space, and when one of us was waiting for the other to violate it by asking a question. We graduated at the same time. I became a graduate assistant at the university, and she moved to Nottingham to work for an interior design company. She came to London to see me every Saturday, while I avoided going to Nottingham for one reason:

I could not take trains.

I had discovered my phobia of trains in the first month after my arrival in London. Friends of some of my Arab friends in London invited me to visit them in Manchester. I bought the ticket and stood waiting at the station. Each time a train passed, whether it was leaving or arriving, I felt nervous. When my train pulled up, I stood in front of the open door for many moments. It was entirely possible that I could have remained standing there, or indeed retreated from boarding altogether, but a large man behind me shoved me inside, telling me to hurry before the door closed automatically. I found myself aboard with my small suitcase. While other people busied themselves arranging their luggage, I was beginning to think of getting off. But before long the train pulled away, and I found myself trapped inside the moving car. I couldn't sit down on the seats like the others. My legs froze. I remained like this, in the space linking one car to another, close to the door. Every time the train stopped I thought about disembarking, but I hesitated when I considered that doing this could make matters even worse. What if I ended up in a small town that didn't have a bus station? What would I do if I couldn't find a bus that would take me to Manchester at the right time? What if a taxi to return to London, or to continue onward, was prohibitively expensive?

I decided to stay where I was. Cold sweat was beginning to soak my shirt. My condition worsened when the train went through tunnels or whenever another train passed on the adjacent track, producing a strange sound as we nearly came into contact. I was nauseous, but my empty stomach prevented me from vomiting. The train would accelerate and then slow suddenly at the approach of the stations where it stopped. On top of my nausea, I began to feel dizzy. My distress increased with every moment. I kept looking from where I stood at the other track running by. I saw the two rails recede and turn away, then draw closer and intersect, before receding again. A pretty woman passed me and asked if there was something wrong. I told her rudely to go away. I was unable to communicate with anyone. My vision was becoming fragmented.

I arrived in Manchester suffering from overwhelming fatigue. I had scarcely introduced myself to the friends of my friends, who were waiting at the station for me, when they saw the state I was in and began inquiring anxiously whether I was okay.

I slept all day. My head was heavy and I had lost my appetite. When I got up, one of my hosts accompanied me to a square in

Manchester. We walked a great distance. The lights of the stores glowed in an unfamiliar way. Everything was colorful. I could smell Belgian cake. The scent was pungent and new to me, I who had no special relationship to scents, to the point where I sometimes did not smell them. I paused in front of the street vendor, devouring two cakes made with bittersweet chocolate, and I felt satisfied for the first time in a while.

I returned to London on the night bus.

Of course, my fear of trains prevented me from discovering many parts of Britain. Buses and planes were the alternative, but the bus didn't go everywhere or took too long, and plane travel usually cost a lot more unless the reservation were made far in advance. My friend Ghali couldn't understand for a moment how I could take planes but wouldn't set foot on a train. I would say to him, "I don't understand either."

The first time I slept with Takara, after she moved in with me, I stopped kissing her, raised my sweaty face, and said in a resolute tone, "Before we go on, you have to know something about me." She looked at me in surprise as she cupped my face in her hands, as if she were expecting a dangerous confession. I told her, "I don't take trains."

She looked at me uncomprehendingly. Then she laughed.

This was not one of my misunderstood jokes. I meant what I said completely. Something inside of me had convinced me: before you sleep with this girl, you have to tell her about your fear. But I laughed along with her, and we continued making love.

Takara had no cause to remember this incident until she suggested to me sometime later that we go to Liverpool by train. My answer was definitive: "By train, no." Only then did she remember, and realize that I hadn't been joking, and that she had been mistaken to laugh.

Once we were married, Takara came to live with me in London. I felt guilty. She had left a job she liked to move where I preferred to be. She made it clear to me, however, that this was her choice, and that I had to quit blaming myself. "I need a break," she said. "I need to spend a little time watching you while I do nothing."

I didn't question her further. Takara had peculiar ways of expressing herself, and I was conscious that her sentences sometimes had more than one side to them, more than one meaning. Even when they seemed quite commonplace at first, they could also, I thought, approach philosophy. It depended on my frame of mind. Perhaps this was an effect of my having studied creative writing and comparative literature?

Takara herself had told me more than once that she saw how I turned all things into the substance of a novel. This was fine, she said, but in my relentless pursuit of doing so I would overlook many aspects of real life.

"Overlook them?"

She explained further. "The things around us are neutral," she said. "On an equal plane. We are the ones who raise them up high or bring them down. Disgust is as we define it. Morality is as we define it too. We define right, and we define wrong. We are obsessed with defining everything external to ourselves. Yet this does not mean that we acknowledge what we have defined. We complicate things and we simplify the relationships among them. We invert the truth. Things are by their nature simple, but they coexist within a circle of complex relationships. You, when you write, complicate things and simplify relationships. A novel is a simplification," she said. "Can you deny it? Even stories that are not trying to provoke social or political changes and are only meant to entertain, most of them simplify the relationships among their characters. Perhaps simplicity in relationships is what we desire in an alternate reality? Even cheap melodramas, we relate to them because they entertain hidden parts of our souls. Do you tell stories to entertain? Is life supposed to be entertaining? You do not know? Maybe? No? It is not important. The important thing is that when you do this all the time and not just when you write, when you see everything as a story, you lose much of the complexity of relationships, and much of the simplicity of things. You are constructing a perfect scene, so you let yourself overlook everything else that has no place in your idea of it."

I stared at her, surprised. Here was a novel right in front of me and I hadn't noticed. I slept with her. I drank. I ate. I walked. I whistled. I sang. But I wasn't paying attention. Was paying attention, for its part, just the starting point of another definition? Was I simplifying with my metaphor when I described Takara as a novel?

I felt my eyes radiating light that day whenever I looked at her. I could see them. My eyes, I mean. She smiled and said to me, "Here you go, constructing your scene again. Where am I now in the scene?" She asked me this and laughed her special Japanese laugh. Then she left me in silence and went to prepare lunch.

When I remember Takara, she appears to me coming from a remote place and time. She has preceded me into the valley while I have remained above, searching for the stone steps so I can descend. In London, Takara created beautiful houses. Each time she opened the door of a house to show me, I was amazed. So many houses that hadn't seemed, from the outside, capable of bearing this beauty within them. Colors. Ceilings. Small items of furniture. Accessories. I began to feel a profound conviction that we were alike in this respect: both of us were constructing our own perfect scenes.

While she left her scenes inside houses, I would submerse myself in the scenes in my head. Yet despite this, I was unable to write a single word of any of the projects I had told my friends I was working on. It was hard on me. My mind was a commotion of thoughts and images, but when I opened my laptop and

أنتَ تروي لتُمتِع

لكن هل الحياة
ممتعة؟

touched my fingertips to its keyboard, everything froze. The cursor stayed blinking at the beginning of the line. I tried to write, and all that came out was scattered words, pathetic sentences. All progress in my head stopped as my thoughts entered an endless revolving cycle of limbo. It's not easy when you manage to get a story published in one of the best culture magazines while you're still a student, and are rewarded for it with a prestigious prize for young writers, and then find out later when you graduate that you are unable to write anything more.

I was the prisoner of my first story. I was incapable of going back and returning to a writing that was fresh and not weighted with the knowledge of what had preceded it, nor could I move forward and incorporate what I had learned into writing something new. Takara would watch me, as was her habit. She would come up behind me and fold me in her embrace, keeping me in her arms for a long time. Sometimes I would fall asleep then and awake to find myself lying on the edge of the bed, listening to her voice outside the room singing in Japanese.

A year passed while we were in London. Things were happening in Lebanon to destabilize the status quo there. Then 2005 passed. 2006 flew by. I began to ask myself, Is it the place? Can I really be productive in a place I've lived in only briefly? Can I write a story whose events take place in Lebanon while I watch what's happening from outside? Can such a thing be done remotely, using online searches, smart technology?

I could not keep my thoughts to myself. I asked Takara, "Will you go with me to Lebanon?"

Her answer surprised me. "Yes, right away."

"We won't be tourists," I said.

She replied, "I know."

Sometimes I don't understand Takara.

We arrived in Beirut. We rented an apartment. She adjusted quickly. I'm not exaggerating when I say that she got to know almost all of the shop owners and workers on our street, in spite of the fact that she didn't speak Arabic and didn't try to learn it. I didn't understand how she communicated with people. More than once I saw her doing it, and each time she was employing a different method, once communicating through acting, once with gestures, once by showing examples, once by drawing in her small notebook, once by speaking English slowly, once by speaking rudimentary French, and once by mixing the two languages. It was she who came up with the idea for the Man-sourieh house. Suddenly, with no preamble, she said that it was a shame that we were paying all this money in rent. We had the means to buy a house, so why not? So we bought it, and she began to paint it from the inside out while I tried to write my novel alone in the apartment.

In my attempts to write the novel, I tried to start chronologically and go from the beginning to the end. But I found myself lost. The scenes would come charging from my head onto the computer screen as if they were bursting through a barrier. At first when the gate opened, everything was fine. I began by transcribing every idea that came to mind, trusting that the picture would become clear soon and then I could rearrange things. I would do that after putting this chaos down in words, I persuaded myself at the time.

But I reached an impasse as soon as we moved to Mansourieh. I again felt distant, even though I went down into Beirut daily. I couldn't identify the reason. Only, everything had stopped. And when I looked at what I had written before, I found it disorganized and impossible to arrange. Fragments suitable for nothing, despite their abundance. I would sit in my office without accomplishing anything, while Takara, in Beirut, rebuilt houses from the inside. She seemed happy to me. She had built a network of relationships quickly since our arrival in the country. None of the events around us had an effect on her. Even the numerous explosions, even the assassinations reported on television. Each thing was discrete, not forming a coherent picture for her.

Again, it seemed to me that she noticed my crisis. This time she chose to leave me alone. Once, as we were preparing to go to sleep, I moved up behind her in the bed and put my arms around her.

"What?" she asked me, turning around.

I gazed into the wide pupils of her eyes. I thought about her family in Japan. My smile broadened. She was waiting for me to speak, but I sufficed with a smile. Then, apparently tired of waiting, she pulled gently away from me, rolled onto her side, and went to sleep. I lay flat again. I stared at the ceiling without doing anything. Perhaps ten minutes passed before I declared, "Let's have a baby."

She was sleeping, and she didn't hear.

The next day, I set off for Beirut. I parked my car in a lot on the outskirts of downtown and walked. I jogged. I ran. My body, unusually for me, was drenched in sweat. I stopped after an hour. I sat on a stone bench near the Raouché rocks. Tourists obscured the famous sight from me, but before long they returned to their bus. The Raouché seemed close, closer than usual. What now? I wondered. Where to from here? We had come from London to Beirut based on my theory that the place was the problem. Yet all I had done here was produce a jumble of chaotic ideas from which I hadn't managed to craft even a single short story. With me, everything stopped before it started. Everything came to an early end. Then I began to ask myself: Has a single thing worthy of being narrated ever happened to me? Do I have a story? And how can someone who doesn't have—at the minimum—even one story write a novel? Or do I have a story and I just don't realize it? And if I have one, how can I train myself to see it?

An elderly photographer approached me. He asked me if I wanted my picture taken. I don't know what expression my sweaty face presented to him, but the photographer thought it was an affirmative answer. I found him standing in front of me asking me to smile, and a minute later he was fanning the air with the printed photo and holding it out for me to take. I paid him what was in my pocket, barely noticing how much I gave him, but he thanked me and moved away, calling gaily, "Photo! Photo!"

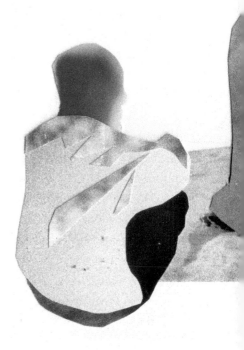

I looked at the picture in my hand. I saw myself as a stranger. Weary shoulders, sweaty face, legs clamped together, a smile taking its time to appear. Was that a smile?

I remembered how I was incapable of crying. I remembered how I had been struggling for days without bringing forth a single tear, and now I couldn't manage a smile either. Neither a smile nor a tear. Where was my mistake? What was it I kept missing?

I returned to the house and seques- tered myself in my office. For a week

I slept on the small sofa there. Takara didn't come near me.
I would hear only the door being opened and closed in the morn-
ings. She gave me my privacy, as usual. Yet as much as I valued
that in her, I hoped at the same time that she would interfere.
I would leave the room to go to the bathroom and return to find
food ready on the desk, without my ever seeing her.

At the end of the week I emerged. My beard had grown out
for the first time in a long while. Takara had never seen me
like this. When she looked at me, disgust appeared on her face.
She muttered something I didn't understand and left the house.
It was the first time I'd heard her mutter like this.

I went into the bathroom to wash my face. My eyes looked sunken, the circles around them dark and alarming. I threw water on my face and chose to leave my beard as it was. I wouldn't trim it yet. I discarded my clothes on the bathroom floor and stood under the shower, turning on the hot water as high as it would go. The water poured down on me, but I couldn't feel its warmth. I thought for a moment that the hot water heater must have broken.

I left the bathroom naked after discovering that I hadn't brought fresh underwear with me. The clothes I'd tossed on the floor had gotten wet. Before I went to my room to dress, I stopped in the hall. Something drew me to the room with glass walls. I headed that way, passing by the TV, which Takara had left on when she went out. The screen was crowded with news headlines and excited announcers. It looked like something serious had happened, but I didn't raise the volume and I didn't pause long enough to understand what.

From the room with glass walls, I gazed out at the green hills below. I thought about making a cup of coffee. I went into the kitchen, prepared it, and returned. I was moving automatically. This was the first time I had walked through the house naked. Not many minutes had passed before I heard the front door bang open. I turned to see Takara before me, crying. She looked at me, and then she asked me to get dressed so we could talk. I said, "We can't talk when I'm like this?" I spoke to her in English, and I felt a sense of calm as a gentle breeze stroked my naked body.

My playfulness was misplaced. Takara exploded. I had never seen her like this. She was transforming before my eyes.

She began to curse me, and to curse the country and the people, and to curse herself. She shouted in Japanese, words I didn't know. I understood her at that moment, though, even without having learned her language. She shouted in English, "I cannot keep doing this! I cannot!"

I made an effort that day to encourage her to say everything she wanted to, and then I left her alone for a little while. I left her in front of the TV watching the live broadcast of the events from Beirut and cursing in Japanese. When I saw that her anxiety was only increasing, I went to turn off the TV. She screamed at me not to. She was smoking cigarettes ravenously, and in front of her the ashtray had filled with a pile of butts. I left the room and went to sleep on my small sofa.

I remained deep in sleep until the afternoon. I awoke to find the nearby wardrobe open. I examined its contents. It seemed that many of Takara's clothes had disappeared.

I was certain of it: she had left the country.

My suspicion was confirmed when I received a text message from her near evening: *On my way to Japan via Damascus airport.* I went into the office, and I remained there reading what I had tried to write in the preceding days. I started by erasing some of it. I was thinking about many things, except about Takara. I wrote. I wrote. I wrote. I couldn't remember ever before producing this quantity of words in a single day. I sat there tapping away at the keyboard, completely naked. I had begun to relish moving through the house without clothes.

Is this the novel I've been waiting for? I wondered. I finished two chapters and started on the third. I didn't sleep. I drank a lot of coffee, cup after cup. At four o'clock in the morning, I stopped and looked at what I had accomplished. Happiness washed over me in spite of my exhaustion.

Naked in the darkness of the room with glass walls, I watched the dance of lights upon the hills, and I began to think. Who had turned Takara into that creature? How could a person defined by her ability to manage everything lose control like this? Was it her certainty that further attempts to help me would only yield more failure? Did Takara fail with me, and did she know that she had failed, and so she exploded? Was it I who pushed her to this state?

Many thoughts assailed me. I paced through the house, colliding with furniture in the darkness. I almost tripped

on a step, and I knocked something over that shattered behind me on the floor. I continued my progress toward my room, not caring whether shards from the broken object might pierce my bare feet. I was terrified by the thought that I had not adequately memorized the map of the house, although Takara had not changed the positions of the furniture since our move.

In my room, I picked up the first shirt and pair of pants that my hands fell upon. I did not look in the mirror. I found myself a few minutes later in the car heading to Beirut. The clock showed that it was nearly five o'clock in the morning. I took the coastal road. Sleep canopied the neighborhoods through which I passed. Only rarely did I happen upon another car. Instead of continuing into Beirut, I took a turn and drove north until I arrived at the neighborhood of El Zouk.

A feeling beset me that I lacked free will, that I was advancing toward an unknown goal awaiting me somewhere. Yet some part of what was in front of me was not wholly unfamiliar. A chaos of thoughts encircled me. I began to think

about scenes from the fourth or fifth chapter of my novel, about lines that needed more work, about characters that asked to be better developed. By the time I reached El Zouk, I had left my novel behind and was focusing in a different direction entirely: Takara.

This was the first time that she had crossed my mind since I abandoned myself to writing. I saw her in the windshield of the car. The heavens rained gently down upon her. It was strange for it to rain in May. I turned on the wipers, but the image did not disappear. Takara's presence intensified, with her narrow black eyes and her smooth hair, and she looked at me in anger. I could no longer recall my characteristic calm image of her.

How can people leave behind them, when they depart, a final image of themselves that erases everything that came before? I wondered. It's illogical. It proves that things are weaker than they seem. But not so fast: Was I speaking here about things, or about the relationships among things? With me, why does everything (simple things and their complicated relationships) become suddenly joined together into one mass?

Does complication overrule simplicity?

I don't know what motivated me to turn around and return in the direction of Beirut. The hour was some minutes past five. I recalled Takara's words in Japanese that I hadn't understood. I translated them into the image before me, into the subtlest facial expression or physical movement I had observed her make during our confrontation. Was it really a confrontation? I had been weak, and she came and let everything out all at once, but

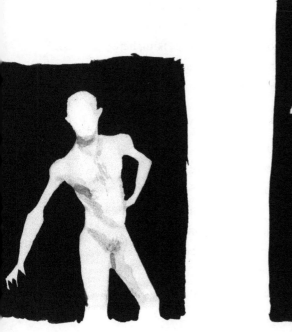

did I blame her? Can one who is not responsible for her own behavior be blamed?

I felt guilty. I became certain that she was my victim. That I was the one who had brought her to the point of explosion. At the head of Hamra Street, which was empty of all life, I could hear the sound of the paving stones bumping against the tires of my car. I entered a side street and then came out again. I no longer remember the route I took. All I remember is that I returned to the main street, and there I stopped. In front of me Takara had begun to scream. She beckoned me forward. I thought that if I drove faster I might throw her image off the glass. I might leave her behind on the sidewalk, on top of one of those little golden stars engraved there.

And she might disappear forever.

I flew.

The bumping of the tires against the paving stones became louder. The din escalated, and Takara continued shrieking in Japanese, and then . . . he appeared in front of me.

A man in dark clothes stood pointing his weapon at a young man. It would have been possible for me to avoid him, but something inside of me convinced me that this must not happen, and that he himself had been waiting for me for a long time. I felt adrenaline throb in my veins, and I awoke from the stupor that had begun to envelop me on the coastal road.

It all happened in seconds.

★   ★   ★

Things take a much shorter time to happen than the period we spend preparing for them on the ground, on paper, or even in our heads. The things we are waiting for often surprise us with their insignificance once they actually come to pass. We ask ourselves, is it for this we were waiting? Is it for this we were planning? The weightiness of such questions eclipses the insignificance of the event itself. When I struck the man with my car, it took time for me to arrive at the weightiness that would follow. My questions about myself and about Takara vanished in an instant. I was within the insignificance, and everything passed through me, and my mind's eye that turns everything into the material for a novel put the event into slow motion.

I can recount what happened in plain facts.

The man clung at first to the hood of the car. He stared into my face. His deep-set eyes hunted for mine. His face was dyed with blood, and blood also flowed from his open mouth. The red fluid covered the glass, obscuring my sight. The man stuck to the car as if he were embracing it and did not wish to let it go. I took him with me. I drove without being able to see past him to the road, aided by the fact that this part of the street does not curve. Then I decided that I needed to see. With my right foot I slammed on the brakes, and the man flew and landed near the middle of the street.

I opened my door and got out. I looked from where I stood to the man crumpled on the asphalt unmoving. I looked behind me for the young man at whom he had been aiming his weapon. I found no one. I surveyed the street. It was calm and devoid of life. I was surprised that no one was out and about yet now that the sun had risen. I looked up. The sky was overcast, and presently rain began to fall into my upturned eyes. As if the sky had been waiting for me to look up. This time it was discharging its burden with violence, unlike the drizzle on the autostrade earlier. I hurried to get in my car without going over to check on the man's condition. I took a side street, careful not to pass near the body. I drove very slowly at first, with no feeling of fear or of a need to flee. I was like a zombie who has had his meal and keeps walking as if he hasn't done anything, or as if what he did was completely natural and he had the right to do it.

The rain had rinsed the windshield clean, and I turned on the wipers again. This time Takara did not appear. It was enough seeing the blood disappearing under the hood. There was lightning and thunder. Had I been thinking normally in those moments, I would have remembered all the cheap details that always accompany a criminal act in works of fiction determined to be obvious about their message: Lightning. Thunder. Rain. The perpetrator runs. He hides. Then he continues his getaway. When he reaches a safe place, he cries. Or he is lashed by pangs of conscience.

But I, contrary to all of this, was driving very slowly, heading toward the Corniche. And except for the details provided by nature and outside my control, I did not do any of what would seem logical in these situations. I had not even reached that post-event feeling of weightiness.

I started to see cars around me. Other militiamen were gathered on the corners, sheltering from the rain under the shop awnings and smoking their morning cigarettes. Not much later I arrived at the Raouché rocks. The rain had lightened again into a drizzle. I parked the car and got out. I looked at the windshield. I found no

trace either of blood or scratches, only a slight dent in the hood that would mean nothing to anyone who happened to notice it.

"You got a cigarette?" I asked one of the few people standing on the Corniche sidewalk. The man gave me one and I put it in my mouth. He took out a lighter for me and we joined our hands together trying to shield the flame from the sea breeze until we succeeded in lighting it.

"This sure is a nice morning," he said to me in the tone of one speaking to a comrade in a secret brotherhood.

For the first time in a while I felt that I had to speak. "Here's to hoping that yours gets even better." I gave him my hand in thanks and went over to the guardrails. I leaned on them and looked out at the heaving sea.

This time the rocks were distant. Very distant.

I waited for a long time without fear, but the photographer did not appear this time.

In the house, when I return, I will check my passport, and I will find that the Japanese visa in it is still good.

At the Syrian–Lebanese border I will smile at the border guard, and he will stamp my passport, and I will give him a pack of Marlboro Reds.

On the plane heading from Damascus to Tokyo I will sleep for most of the flight.

My friend Ghali will come to me in a dream and repeat what he said to me: "Everything's mizyan, my friend, it's fine." I will see a train passing through me. I will smell many smells. Each smell will overflow into another. I will see a strange Japanese tattoo on the chest of a man, and I will be certain in the dream that I do not know him. All the writers I like to read will visit me, and the train will keep passing through me but I will not feel any shortage of breath. I will feel only a sense of alienation.

Only when the hostess puts her hand on my shoulder, whispering to me that we have arrived, will I awake. In the Tokyo airport, I will call Takara from a public phone. I will not say much. I will wait for her in the arrivals hall, and an hour will pass before she appears. She will stand there at first, and then she will run toward me and embrace me, and I will hear her crying, and as usual I will not be able to shed a single tear.

In bed, I will hold her. I will ask her to have a child with me. She will listen to me and smile, and then she will say, *On the condition that we give it a Japanese name*, and I will nod in agreement, and kiss her. As we are making love, I will not see Takara's face. Speeding trains will overtake my vision, and I will verge on suffocation. But I will not show her that I am suffocating. I will cry for the first time, as I try to suppress my feeling of suffocation, and I will get the cheap scene that I managed to postpone

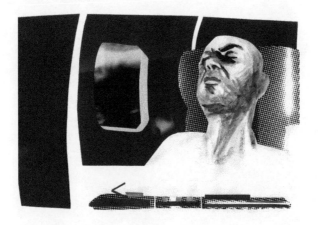

before. Takara will ask me if there's something wrong, and I will answer in the negative, and I will get control of myself, and I will continue making love.

But the bloodstain will keep growing in my head, and I will see him. I will see his eyes again, and I will think about him. I will give him a definition: he is the first story that has happened to me. My strength will give out as I arrive inside Takara's womb.

Before I close my eyes, I will remember that I forgot my laptop, and on it the first chapters of my novel, in the house in Mansourieh. And instead of wondering whether I will return there, or thinking of a way to recover the device, I will find myself haunted by a peculiar question: What child did we just create, while I could not stop thinking about the man I killed?

I will not find an answer to my question. At least not before nine months have passed. For now I will close my eyes, and I will enjoy a little bit of darkness, and a quantity of strange dreams.

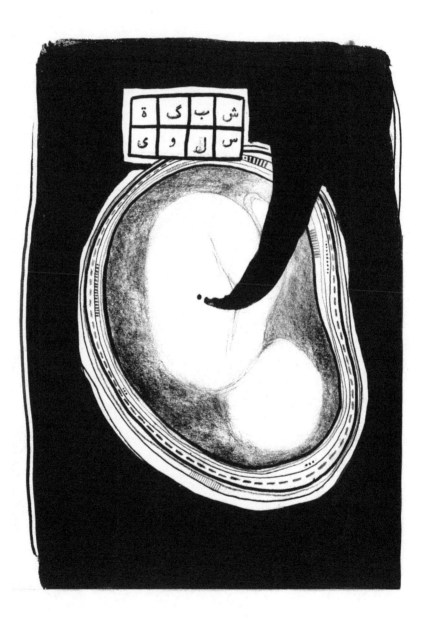

3

Salwa's Puzzle

ILLUS. JANA TRABOULSI

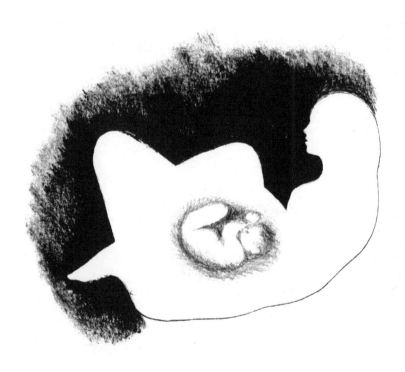

EXHAUSTED THOUGH SHE WAS, Salwa would not be prevented from getting out of the car as soon as she spotted the magazines through the window. Immediately, she asked her driver to stop.

"Madame, we can't stop here," Abu Jerji said.

Without knowing quite how, Abu Jerji found himself opposite a narrow lane that was not heavily trafficked, and Salwa asked him to pull over in front of it.

"Stop here and turn on the flashers. I'll be right back."

In vain the elderly driver tried to make her understand that he couldn't stop the car here, and that if he did, he could get a fine.

The Madame's answer was, "If the police come, keep going. Turn around and come back. I won't be long. I'll be waiting by the newspaper kiosk."

Salwa climbed out and started walking without looking back. This was the first time this week that she had been able to get down from the high 4x4 without feeling pain. Her belly was light, and the little man had not kicked her when she stood up. She paused at the corner. The traffic was light enough that the cars were traveling quickly, and this made the crossing more difficult than it would have been at another time. She gripped the base of her belly with her right hand and with her left she gestured to the cars to stop. She had found herself making this motion—putting her hand under her stomach—since the sixth month of her pregnancy. She didn't know why. To others, it seemed as if she were preventing her child from sliding out of her, as if she were keeping him within her.

At last the driver of an old white *service* taxi stopped for her. He nodded to her, indicating that she should go. No sooner had Salwa crossed in front of the *service* when another car came speeding up beside it and almost slammed into her. The driver hit the brakes. Salwa moved fast enough to avoid being struck directly, but the car still made contact with her and flung her to the curb on the other side of the street. It happened in the blink of an eye. Even Abu Jerji did not realize what had occurred until he heard the uproar in the street and poked his head out of the car window to see a crowd forming.

He raced over to find the Madame lying prostrate on the ground, although she had not lost consciousness. It was as if she had simply fallen over where she was standing. Her eyes were open but did not blink, and her hand was still on the same part of her belly. People were asking her not to move and trying to find out whether she was in any pain. Two middle-aged women stood looking down at her where she lay at their feet.

They were checking the ground underneath her to make sure there was no liquid coming from her.

Salwa could not see anything at that moment except the sky, a clear blue without clouds. She barely registered the faces of those assembled around her. The voices grew hushed for several seconds, and then Abu Jerji's face appeared above her. He was talking to someone on the phone. She also saw an anxious man whom she did not recognize. If she had been paying a little more attention as she was crossing the street, she would have known that the anxious face belonged to the driver who had hit her.

These few moments of consciousness were followed by a new kind of clarity, this time black.

★   ★   ★

Connecting Words: To solve the following challenges, start from the arrow and work in a counterclockwise direction.

Where did Salwa's thoughts start when consciousness returned to her? She could not find the right place to begin. In her mind, she tried and she failed. Whenever she decided that this was the word she would begin with, numerous other words attacked her. She could not cross off any of the possibilities. Everything exploded, swimming inside her head and before her eyes as they carried her. At first she could feel the directions: right, left, forward, stop, an elevator, a door opening. She struggled to maintain her focus, but she lost her ability to do so after a few minutes. Although she was certain that her injury was not dangerous, a powerful fatigue overtook her. Maybe it was the fatigue of nearly nine months of pregnancy? Maybe it was her mother, and her husband, and her family, and everything her mother did not know about her, that was causing it? Her weariness was like a wave, coming and going, and whenever she woke up she felt like she was either losing part of herself or someone was putting something inside of her.

She didn't know how much time passed in this way. When she opened her eyes again, all she could see was white. She concentrated a little and moved her gaze a few degrees to the right to find a bright light shining above her. She was looking at the ceiling of a hospital room. Her guess was confirmed when her left hand touched the arm of a bed. She raised her own arm with difficulty to discover an IV fixed in it. She realized how weightless she felt and directed her gaze at once to her stomach. It was still huge, the huge belly of a pregnant woman. She stretched both hands under the blanket and touched it. It felt swollen as usual, but she wanted more information. She touched every part of it. She searched for the child inside of her until she found him. She didn't know how to describe what her hands felt, but she knew that he was crouching there. She almost smiled, but then she realized that she did not feel any movement. She began to walk her hands over her rounded stomach. Maybe the little boy would kick her. She had convinced herself that whenever she did this it tickled the boy. This time she couldn't detect anything. She began to cry uncontrollably.

"The boy is fine."

Salwa heard her mother's voice. She tried to raise her head, but the bed was not in a position to allow her to see the whole room. A few seconds later her mother's face appeared above her.

She handed Salwa a tissue so she could wipe her tears before they left visible marks, and she said, "The doctor said everything's fine, and that you shouldn't worry if you feel like the boy isn't moving."

Her mother stood up as though preparing to leave, but instead of leaving she launched into one of her usual lectures. Salwa nodded affirmatively. She was not in agreement with what her mother was saying so much as she was trying to keep the speech brief, although she knew that her mother would not stop

talking until she had expressed all of her opinions, instructions, the steps she thought Salwa should take . . . so Salwa let her relieve herself of everything that was on her mind. She listened to the reproaches, and to the questions about why she had left the house, and to the threats against Abu Jerji, who had disobeyed his orders, and to the repeated thanks to God that her husband was out of the country, and to the request, or rather the demand, that she pay a friendly visit to her husband's family as soon as her health improved, or else.

"I won't tell them. The doctor said two days, then you can go home. Anyway, they won't stop by the house to check on you, and Abu Jerji won't say anything. I'll tell them you came to stay with me for a couple of days. Thank the Lord your husband is traveling."

Salwa was barely listening to her mother. She was looking away and recalling what had brought her here. She remembered the newspaper kiosk and what she had seen there. It was all in fragments. She imagined transforming her mother's words into scrambled letters within squares, with arrows beside them. Whenever her mother mentioned a key word—*husband*, for example—Salwa chose the correct letters with her eyes and placed them in their proper squares, and then she went back and crossed them out in their previous positions. She played this game on an imaginary screen to escape her mother's nagging.

She kept at it until they heard a knock at the door. Abu Jerji stood outside. Her mother did not wait long before hurling yet another remonstrance at the old man. "What are you doing here? Didn't I tell you to stay in the car?"

"I came to check on the Madame."

"To check on her? You could have thought for one second instead and let her out by the sidewalk instead of making her cross the street."

"I swear to God, ma'am . . . it all happened so fast."

"Stop, stop! *Khalas!* Enough of this talk. Go back to the car. I want you to drive me somewhere in a little while."

Before the man could turn to leave, Salwa called out to him. He went to her and she gestured to him to bend down close to her. She whispered something in his ear and he nodded his head several times. The conversation was taking place right in front of her mother, who seemed to be fuming with rage but to be making an effort not to show it. She knew her daughter. She knew her daughter well, and she knew her purpose in behaving like this. The man made ready to leave, saying, "Anything for you, Madame." He headed for the door, but as he had expected, Salwa's mother overtook him with a new threat.

"Abu Jerji! I'm not done with you yet."

The man nodded and left the room.

Now, as Salwa had anticipated, the second phase of her mother's scolding campaign began. This time she removed herself completely. She would not listen to her. *She would not listen to her.* She would pass the time inside her game. She would sink even deeper into it. In her mind she would choose a harder puzzle, and she would begin to solve it.

★ ★ ★

Clue: The four-letter name of an ancient Canaanite god of the sea.

Clue: An Umm Kulthum song, eight letters long, based on a mel⌐⌐*Riyad El Sunbati.*

When Salwa spied the magazines from inside the car, she realized that she might have discovered what could restore to her a long-ago time she had thought was gone forever. She could not have explained her discovery to her mother or even to Abu Jerji. Abu Jerji did things for her; her mother fought with her. That was it.

Or perhaps it was she who fought with her mother?

But what if someone else asked her? How would she reply? She would need an answer someday, certainly. Or even if she never did, didn't she need to explain it to herself at least? So where should she start? With the four-letter name of the sea god? Or would she end there? Should she start with the Umm Kulthum song? How should she fill in the puzzle?

She would try. She would say that there are small things. Details that seem trivial to some to the same extent that they seem important to others. And perhaps, going further, she might elaborate and compare these things to songs which give their listener special pleasure by making him believe that they are sung especially for him, or which bring back to him certain images and moments from past events until they all but transport him to the very location where the events took place, so that he feels the same desire he did then, smiles the same smile, finds the same expressions on his face. Sometimes, the event itself cannot even be recalled. Sometimes, the only thing brought back is those expressions.

Like someone listening to one of these songs, Salwa does not take in the words right away. She focuses on the melody first. The melody is the surrounding atmosphere. The external form. The wrapping paper. It is like an addiction. If she likes a thing or a person, she lets herself dissolve into that thing or person to the point where it becomes a passion, to where it becomes an essential part of herself. Afterward, only afterward, does she realize what has happened and attempt to analyze the situation.

This is how Salwa is. Whenever she saw a magazine of word games, she was brought back to her teenage years in the 1980s

when she used to collect such magazines. She used to smile every time she saw her name in the title of one of them: *Salwa*. At the time, she barely noticed the second word that followed her name: *Puzzles*. She had great faith in her favorite theory, which maintained that this magazine was her magazine. Hers alone. And when she finally noticed the word *Puzzles*, it did not undermine her theory but rather supported it. She said to herself: "This is my puzzle. These puzzles inside are my puzzles." The discovery was merely a trivial detail to her.

The first person who noticed her interest in crossword puzzles was her father. She would rip out the portion of the newspaper that contained the games section, and she wouldn't lift her head from it until she had solved all the puzzles. Her father would always come to reclaim the page from her eventually, although often he waited until she was finished with it.

The reverse side of the games section included the continuation of the front-page news, with the lead articles and official opinion pieces for the newspaper, all of which her father read avidly.

Sometime after that, her father discovered magazines dedicated entirely to word games and puzzles. She can never forget the day when he entered the house carrying five issues at once and called her over, and when she came, he presented them to her, saying, "I brought you *Salwa*, Salwa."

This is one of the moments that Salwa replays in her memory whenever she picks up a magazine of this type. Whenever she raises one of them in front of her, her father comes again to offer her those five issues. Extending his hands to her in the same way. It is the same moment in time. As if it had happened yesterday.

As if he had just closed the door behind him and gone out, and she could hear the sound that the soles of his black shoes made as they knocked against the few steps at the entrance of the house. As if he had returned to her holding a rolled-up newspaper and cursing the militants who were all over the streets.

In short, *Salwa's Puzzles* had become her archive of that period. She wouldn't be exaggerating if she said that these magazines were the war for her. These puzzles, which were published with a bewildering numerical sequence of issue numbers on their covers, and without a publication date, disappeared from the market completely after 1991. Salwa's father could no longer get them for her. He began to buy old issues for his daughter, but she would not solve old crosswords. She even had all the prior issues saved in a drawer of her wardrobe. Why should she solve what she had already solved before?

Can a puzzle be solved more than once?

Salwa did not understand how magazines that had continued to be put out at the height of the civil war would stop being published just as peace was near. How could someone who had continued production under the most challenging security conditions — gathering his editors, creating crosswords with different words that were never repeated across issues, printing and distributing the magazine — stop only a short while before the end of the war? Had he simply lost the energy?

She had searched for an answer and not found one, so as was her custom she had resorted to inventing a theory only she believed. She decided that the era for consuming these magazines had ended with the approach of an end to the conflict, when other types of entertainment would become available. That the lifespan of these magazines was the same as the lifespan of the war. They grew up with it, and they would die when the military phase of it was over. And since this magazine had been unsuccessful in claiming a new identity for itself to go along with the next phase, it was natural that it should stop.

In this way Salwa convinced herself.

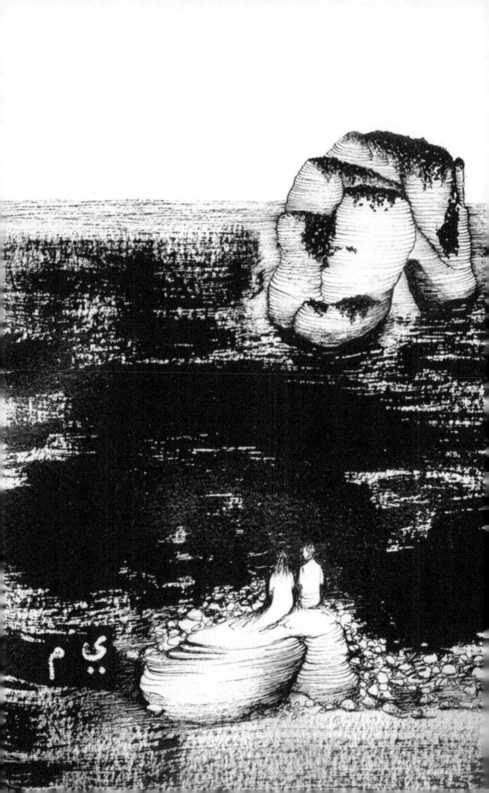

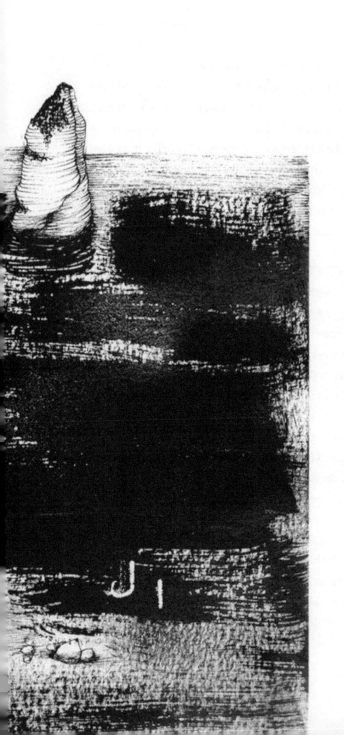

In the nineties, although the magazine had ceased publication, the old issues kept being printed, or counterfeited — Salwa did not know which of the two possibilities was closer to the truth. She was certain at least that the issues were old from the old pictures of the illustrators on the covers and from the number recorded in the left-hand corner of each magazine cover, for she had memorized the number of the last issue: #458. At first she continued to see the magazines set out for sale on the sidewalks and hanging in nylon bags at the newspaper kiosks around Beirut. Then they disappeared altogether. Only a few remained on racks in barbershops and in the waiting rooms at doctors' offices. She would find them with yellowed pages, torn covers. She would open them to discover puzzles that many people had tried and failed to solve, abandoning them after adding a few letters to the boxes with their BIC pens. Maybe the way they were printed and the quality of the paper did not encourage most people to respect them, she thought. She would check them, and make sure that they were old with a quick glance at the interior pages. She recognized the old puzzles as soon as she looked at them. This was a skill she had acquired with the passing of years.

But what happened when she saw the magazines from the window of the car? What was she thinking about as she was crossing the street during the moments before the collision? Did she craft a new theory to believe in? Did she see the beach at Ramlet El Baida? Did she watch the cars stopping along the Corniche, did she hear Umm Kulthum singing? Did she walk ahead of her father, as he held her arms, into the sea? Did they turn around so that she could see smoke rising behind them from the streets of Beirut?

What did Salwa see?

First answer: Yamm.
Second answer: "Memories."

★ ★ ★

Clue: Rearrange the scrambled letters to form a meaningful word.

One day, Salwa woke up and went into the bathroom. She peed.
She felt a burning sensation. She was anxious. Her menstrual
cycle was late. She wandered through the villa, which was empty
except for some servants. She checked the voicemail and text
messages on her cell phone. There were no messages from her
husband. This hadn't concerned her before, but this time she
needed to hear something from him—or indeed, from anyone.

It was complicated.

She did not hate her husband. Perhaps she had hated him in
the beginning. Perhaps before the beginning.

No; she should reformulate this idea.

She had been unconvinced. She came to marriage after
passing through stages that progressed from total refusal (in
which she was supported by her father), to derision whenever
her mother broached the subject, to condescending to meet
suitors before rejecting them, to meeting a suitor more than
once, to choosing among three.

Her father's death further persuaded her to give in. Her
mother's pressure on her was increasing, and she herself was

getting older, and their financial situation was worsening. They had nothing left except the reputation of her mother's family (this is what her mother would say). Her father had come from moderate means, unlike his wife, who was from one of the Achrafieh families known for their wealth.

Salwa hadn't understood how her mother, who had picked her own husband from outside her small social circle, could push her toward the most traditional choice. Had her mother changed after her father's death? No. She had been like this before he died. Her personality had contained this capacity for irritability for a long time. Was it the humble lifestyle that her father had only just managed to provide for the two of them after his death that exacerbated her mother's state? Perhaps. Salwa could find no other reason for the increase in her mother's irritability. She searched without success for other explanations.

When her mother told her for the first time about the man who would become her husband, she had said about him, "He's from an important, well-to-do family, so don't let this one slip through your fingers. And his father is in politics. What more do you want?" This introduction provoked Salwa into deciding in advance to refuse the suitor. Her experiences with the men her mother had introduced her to before did not promise a positive outcome. She had reached the point where she would meet them in person and then send them away, and she resolved to do the same thing with the new candidate.

Her mother told her that they had been invited to a getting-to-know-you luncheon with the suitor's family and that she had to have her hair done. She dropped Salwa off at the *coiffeur* and said that she would return to pick her up after attending to some urgent business so that they could go to the lunch together.

At the hairdresser's, Salwa sat on the chair and looked into the mirror. She saw her hair being volumized, then pulled back, then combed in different ways, then given a complete styling treatment. She watched her appearance change. It took an hour before she was ready, and then she sat on one of the leather chairs in the reception area and waited. She phoned her mother and asked her where she was. She replied that she was coming. A quarter of an hour passed before one of the salon staff called over to her to say that the car parked in front of the shop was waiting for her. Salwa gathered her belongings and went out.

She saw her mother's car with its tinted glass double-parked outside. She hurried toward it, opened the door, and climbed in.

But her mother was not in the car. Instead, she found a young man dressed in athletic clothes. She apologized in embarrassment for the mistake and almost got out again, but the young man, seeming to have anticipated that she would try to leave, addressed her by name.

"Salwa. Your mother sent me. She's at our house right now."

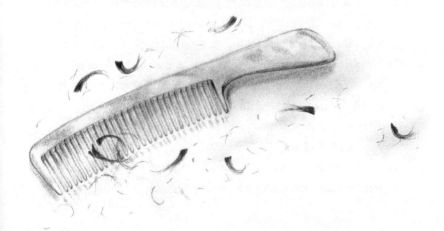

Salwa was confused. She closed the door. He introduced himself to her. Was it him, or was he a different member of the family? His name did not mean anything to her. Her mother had not told her his name. She had mentioned only his last name. Anyway, her mother was not interested in his name. She regarded him only as the son of his family.

On the way, the young man began to talk. He said that everyone was waiting and that the lunch table had been set. Salwa maintained her silence, while she wondered, Is this him? But he seems so young!

After several minutes of talking nonstop, the young man asked in a jesting tone, when he noticed her confusion, "Does my talking bother you?"

Salwa's confusion increased. She began to say something but stopped. The young man laughed, and she asked him why he was laughing.

"There's no need for all this awkwardness," he said. "It's not like we're getting married!"

So it's not him, she concluded in her head.

But he went on, as though reading her thoughts, "No. Don't take it that far. I'm the suitor . . . but we're not getting married."

Salwa did not understand, but she did not ask him to explain. He cursed a car in front of him, then he apologized to her, then he laughed some more, then he spoke with someone on his cell phone, continuing to chuckle audibly as he did so. The young man's merriment was surely excessive.

Salwa. Did not. Understand.

When they arrived at the luncheon, her mother came forward to thank the young man for his kindness in getting her daughter from the *coiffeur*. The young man replied that it had been no trouble.

"Well?" her mother demanded next. "Did you two talk?" It was one of those stupid questions always asked of couples in arranged marriages.

The young man laughed and turned to Salwa. "You should ask Salwa! Well, Salwa? Did we talk?"

Salwa smiled and nodded yes, and her mother laughed heartily before excusing herself and her daughter, telling the young man that she was going to introduce Salwa to some of the other members of the family.

For Salwa, the next few minutes were a blur. She remained quiet apart from exchanging a few polite words with the family members. She decided to go into the house and help prepare the table, but her mother and her "mother-in-law" soon fetched her back outside, saying that there were servants enough to manage the task.

Salwa escaped again and began to wander through the villa, every corner of which was filled with artwork and statues. She paused behind a pair of colored glass doors to watch the young man in the garden as he drank a glass of red wine and spoke with another young man, laughing all the while. She asked herself: Doesn't this guy ever stop laughing?

She made up her mind. She had to understand. She could not leave the puzzle unresolved. She went to stand near him and ordered a glass of wine from the server at the bar. When he noticed her presence, he excused himself from his friend and approached her. He asked the server to pour more wine in his own glass, which was almost empty.

As he waited for his drink, he asked her, "Well? Did you come here to talk to me?"

"Huh?"

"You were over there before—I saw you come over here."

"For wine!" She justified herself by raising her glass.

"Meaning, you don't want to talk to me?"

Salwa looked at him and said, "I would if you weren't so annoying . . . I don't understand you." He laughed, so Salwa adopted a more serious tone. "Maybe you could stop laughing and help me understand."

The young man's countenance took on a more neutral expression when he realized that she meant what she said. He extended his arm, inviting her to come with him. Salwa remained stiff, her irritation plain on her face. (*Did she look like her mother at that moment?* The thought flashed through her mind.)

Noticing her chilly demeanor, he added, continuing to hold his arm out to her, "I apologize. Let me explain. After you."

Salwa went with him, and he explained everything to her.

★ ★ ★

Clue: A famous tourist site at the Beirut beach.

The young man was strange. He did not want to get married; he was only fulfilling the role demanded of him. Just like her. He said that his problem was that he was his parents' only son, which put him under doubled pressure.

"Don't talk to me about pressure," Salwa replied.

While they toyed with their families' nerves, they were in fact becoming an ideal couple. They made a habit of meeting at regular intervals with a group of friends without their families' knowledge. Salwa's mother kept waiting for a phone call from his parents that didn't come. All signs, however, seemed to forecast a lasting friendship and nothing more. The young man did not take any "bold" steps, although he was usually in good spirits. He was like any young man in his early twenties — except that he had already reached the age of thirty-seven. When Salwa found out how old he really was, she was stunned. She accused him of lying. He pulled out his ID card for her and said, "It's the exercise! I swim every day, even in the winter! Outside, inside . . ." He added, laughing, "Wherever I am . . . I swim!"

The situation went on like this for more than two months, during which Salwa's mother returned to her customary irritability. She leveled the most malicious accusations at her daughter, the same ones she had worn out from use each time a suitor escaped. But Salwa did not care, and she did not listen.

After two more months, she went out with him and other friends one night to a nightclub on Sodeco Street. As usual, he left her at the bar and went to meet other people. More than one man approached to talk to her. She brushed them off. She didn't know why. She was following him with her eyes. That night, he was not laughing. He was drinking a lot and exchanging his empty glasses for full ones with unusual speed.

It seemed like he was trying to get revenge for something.

Not two hours had passed before a great weariness seemed to grip him. Salwa stood up and together with some of his friends dragged him out of the middle of the crowd. He resisted them and cursed loudly at everyone around him. They took him outside to the street. She stayed with him along with two of his other friends. He vomited on the curb in front of them. Salwa asked his friends to go back inside and carry on with their evenings. She would stay with him and bring him home, she said. They asked her if she was sure. She nodded yes.

For ten minutes he continued to bring up everything that was in his stomach. Each time he swayed on his feet she caught hold of him. She found him light. Lighter than she would have expected. When he stopped vomiting, she tried to direct him to the car. At first his legs resisted, but then presently they complied. On the way, he kept repeating apologies to her like a small boy. When they arrived, she asked him for the keys. He looked at her with drowsy eyes and did not reply. She laid him gently against the hood of the car and searched his back pockets, but she did not find anything except a wallet. She took it out and began to go through it. She found credit cards and identification and money. She opened an interior pocket fastened with a button and found a condom in it. She closed the pocket and looked at him lying there half-conscious. Then she noticed another small pocket in the front of his pants, and felt inside it, and found the key.

She opened both doors of the car. She called out to him, but he did not reply. In the interim he had fallen asleep against the hood. She tugged on his hands and tried to prop him up. He opened his eyes halfway. She told him, "We need to get in the car."

"Yeah. Yeah. I'll drive," he said.

She ignored his words, put him in the passenger seat, and closed the car door. She got in through the other door and started the engine. While she ran the defroster and waited until the fog lifted from the windshield and the view cleared, she looked at him slumped in the seat unconscious.

He was different. He was not laughing.

They drove. They were close to his home now. As soon as they arrived, Salwa realized that she had a problem. Could she bring him inside at this hour, into his parents' house? With him in this state? She didn't know what to do. She did not know another apartment to take him to.

She stared at him until her eyelids grew heavy.

So they slept in the car.

After a few hours, Salwa awoke to the sound of him vomiting. She looked at her watch and found that it was eight a.m. Her mother would be going crazy, she knew. But she could deal with her, no problem. She got out of the car. She found him standing with his back turned.

She waited for him for several minutes before he came back, wiping his mouth with a tissue.

"I'm really sorry."

Salwa did not reply. He drove them, assuring her that he was fine now. They returned to the Beirut Corniche. He parked the car for a few moments at the Beirut Café and got out. He returned with a coffee for each of them, a bottle of water, and an envelope of Panadol. He placed his cup of coffee next to him in the slot on the dashboard and opened the bottle of water, and then he took two Panadol pills out of the envelope and swallowed them.

He pulled over by the sidewalk on the ocean side of the Corniche and invited her to accompany him. They descended the fishermen's steps cautiously. They sat underneath, on the stone ledge. It was the first time in a while that Salwa had been this close to the sea. She was happy, without letting him see that she was. She did not even care that the skirt of her nice dress might get dirty from sitting on the stones. One of the fishermen noticed them. He came over to them with two small chairs. He wished them good morning and then returned to his fishing pole.

They stayed there for a few minutes drinking what was in their cups. The air, laden with sea spray, stroked their faces. Salwa did not speak, but she looked at him more than once. He kept his eyes fixed on the sea. As she followed his movements out of the corner of her eye, she remembered her father. She recalled the name of the sea god from the crossword puzzle. Yamm. For the first time, *Yamm* meant more to her than *sea*. It was no longer just a word in a puzzle. It had escaped. Flown. Become more than that. The four letters, sealed at the end with the doubled *m*, made the whole thing come into focus. She pronounced it in her head, *Yamm*. She said to herself, This was the original word, not *sea*. She resolved that this was so as she observed him and listened to the sound of the gulls shrieking overhead.

He apologized again. "I'm really sorry."

Salwa did not reply this time either, and he did not wait for her to answer. He returned his gaze to the waves, which had begun to grow larger and pelt them with more spray. He stayed like this for a few more minutes. Then he turned to her. She did not know why he was looking at her like that. She almost asked him, but he spoke first.

"Will you marry me?"
Salwa did not understand.
She did not. Understand.

Answer: the Raouché.

★   ★   ★

Clue: A famous two-word phrase from an Abdel Halim song, written by a celebrated Syrian poet.

How can she summarize multiple months in a few sentences? Why isn't it possible to condense memories into a word or two like in her puzzles? How does time pass? How does it slow down? How does it stretch? How does it become compressed in her mind?

Salwa asked herself these questions often.

She did not accept his marriage proposal. He kept pursuing her for a month. He said that he could not explain everything, but that she could be certain it had nothing to do with family pressure. He was the one asking for her hand. "Me," he said. He elaborated further, but she was not convinced. He had not shown her any romantic interest, so then why did he now want her for his life partner? He tried more than once to justify his proposal. He explained that he was different. "You won't be my life partner," he said. "I won't be your life partner." These were clichés. They meant one person taking possession of another. "We won't be like that."

He tried to explain, but he never really said anything. Explaining without explaining? He would muse aloud in spiraling loops of words that circled and paused, rose and fell without end, without Salwa ever understanding what he meant. His vortex of words continued for a month, before he announced to her that now he would give her space to think. He emphasized that he had to be clear. If she accepted him, this would mean accepting everything he had told her previously. "We'll be . . . different," he said. "I won't interfere. You won't interfere. I've gotten used to living like this. So let's try."

Try? This word would have been guaranteed to dispense quickly with any traditional bride-to-be. But Salwa was also . . . different. Salwa felt that with him she was facing a crossword puzzle of the most difficult sort. It was a challenge. Playing with her future and her life to challenge herself? No!

The idea did not come to her right away. But then it preoccupied her more and more during the period when they were out of contact. Something was missing from her days now. It hadn't been like this before. As usual she needed an excuse to convince herself of the thought she'd had. She began to recall what he had said. She analyzed his words until she had convinced herself. And then, only then, did she phone him and say, "Yes."

After a wedding that all of Beirut knew about — in which the son of a well-known political family was joined in marriage with an attractive young woman from a regular family with distinguished origins — the "different" part began.

Salwa often remembered the first weeks of their marriage. The young man really was different. During sex, for example, he never talked. Sometimes he would bury his head in her shoulder, and at times he would smile his smile that was like the rising sun when his eyes met hers. Even his moans were subdued and lacking in any of the words usually uttered during love-making. She never once heard him use a dirty word. She began to yearn for him to surprise her with some variation in their sex. But their love-making remained resolutely within the borders of tenderness. She would search each time for any difference from the previous occasion, and she never found one.

How could she describe it? It was as if she were solving the same puzzle every time. Each time she solved it, she made fewer mistakes than the time before. Each time she discovered an easier route to the solution. She knew the end was close. Soon she would solve the puzzle without making any mistakes, without having to go back to cross out wrong letters and exchange them for others. What would she do afterward? Copy out the solution again? And what would she do after the first copy? Make a second copy?

Two weeks after the wedding—these first two weeks were their honeymoon, during which he stayed away from his desk and his papers—he began to be absent from the house. Then she felt the burning sensation when she peed. Not long after, her doctor told her she was pregnant. When she told her husband, he was delighted. Thrilled. His smiles multiplied and his laughter diminished. This was an equation that Salwa had never understood: How was his joy translated into silent smiles, while he filled up the empty spaces in his day with laughter? This seemed to her contrary to the way things were supposed to progress from least to most, from the lowest in volume to the loudest, from the usual to the exceptional.

Salwa's body changed. She would stand in front of the mirror and look at herself naked. At the new shape that her

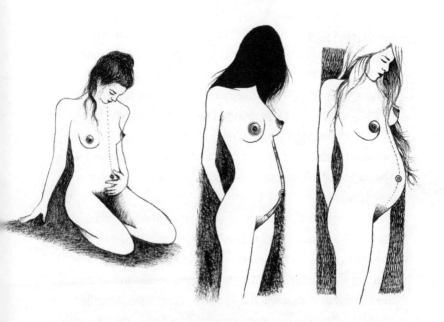

breasts and stomach took on. At the curvature of her back. She saw a new version of herself. In the beginning, she was afraid. But then her husband would come to her and embrace her from behind. He would hold her, or lean down in front of her to kiss her stomach, and this was sure to make her forget her fear of what was coming.

He really was different. He did not ask to have sex with her while she was pregnant. On the contrary, it was she who would ask for it, and he who would refuse. "For the sake of the child," he would say. It didn't seem logical. The doctor permitted it, and they hadn't had sex in weeks, so why wasn't he interested? As usual, she conducted an analysis of the situation. He had found his pretext not to sleep with her. Perhaps the reason for the gentleness of their sex was that he did not enjoy it? This is what Salwa decided.

In spite of all this, she never argued with him. He could absorb and neutralize any sign of a disagreement with a smile or a tender gesture. She did not understand him and she did not understand herself. She longed sometimes to see him outside of this image, to try being annoyed with him like a wife in any normal couple would be, to send him a text message demanding to know why he was late. She didn't know how to do any of this. She respected his announcement that he was different, but she was drowning.

During his absences, she would curl up in a ball naked in the bed, her thighs hugging her distended belly, and think about how many other human beings were lying like her in this position and waiting for sleep to come to them, moist and glistening like the waves of Yamm at the Raouché. Time would lengthen and slow when she was alone in her double bed in the large villa her mother-in-law had given her. If she had wanted to summarize what she was feeling, she would have said simply that she was failing to solve the puzzle.

Answer: "I'm Drowning."

★   ★   ★

Clue: To learn the secret word, you must solve the challenges below before looking for the word you want.
Note: It's best to cross off the words from longest to shortest.

Morning had just broken. Salwa got up from the bed, pulled back the curtain from the window, and looked out into the courtyard of the hospital. She saw a pigeon walking unhurriedly along the edge of the yard and letting out its deep cry. She reached for the bottle of water on the stand next to the bed and gulped down half its contents. She was always parched and thirsty these days. As she returned the bottle to its place, her eyes encountered the pile of puzzle magazines that she had asked Abu Jerji in a whisper to bring her on the first day. The magazines sat there but she had made no attempt to open them. She had ended up here because she was so excited to get her hands on these magazines, and now she had no interest in them. How could she explain it, once again? Indeed, how could she explain many things?

She was tired of explaining.

She continued looking at the magazines without daring to open them to confirm whether they were new or old. She knew from the illustrators pictured on their covers that the copies were probably reprints of past issues. But she wasn't sure. She was protecting herself from another disappointment.

She yanked the IV needle from her arm, picked up her husband's iPod, which Abu Jerji had also brought her, and left her room without notifying anyone. The corridors were calm. She didn't go near the area where the nurses were gathered. She walked in the opposite direction until she reached the elevator. She got in and pressed the button for the ground floor, and then she put the earphones in her ears. She watched the floor numbers light up in descending order.

Despite what her mother had said, her personal doctor had decided to keep her in the hospital for a week. He said that her due date was approaching and it was best that she stay for observation. Over the past few days, she had heard the voices and watched the television news. She switched off the screen, but the voices did not turn off. More than once she stood by the window and looked out to find that the birds had vacated the courtyard and rooftops. She did not know where they went or why they had returned today. She was too exhausted to invent another one of her theories to explain the disappearance of the pigeons. In recent days, the distant, suppressed voices, and the red streaks that appeared now and then in the night sky, had been enough for her. Everything was at a reduced volume. Everything.

Her husband did not send her a single text message. She spoke with her mother and Abu Jerji only on the phone. For their safety, she had asked them not to come. In this country, no one knows what's taking place on the street until he sets foot on it, and when he does, anything at all could happen. Salwa knew this well. She had learned it from the civil war, the final portion of it, to be exact, when her father left the house on a minor errand and never made it back alive.

Yesterday, she had heard about a family with two sons killed on the street. The first son was killed close to the location of the clashes, while the second was killed as he was taking his brother in the car to the hospital. She did not want something like this to happen. The last thing she needed now was another tragedy that defied the rule of logic.

But she wanted to talk, and she could not find anyone to talk to, so she walked. She had persuaded herself that moving was a way of conversing with those who were not present.

The nurses were being kept busy between the floor where her room was and the emergency room. In the elevator, Salwa held up her cell phone and looked at her husband's number. His picture appeared next to it. As always he looked like he was laughing, even though the picture was motionless. This was his laugh, not his smile. She almost began to cry as she felt the child kick her from within.

The last time they had spoken face to face was when she and Abu Jerji drove him to the airport, before her accident. When what happened in Beirut after his departure happened, he called her and asked her if she was all right, and he told her that the roaming feature on his phone was not working for some reason. He cursed the Lebanese telecommunications company. He asked her, "Are you okay, Salwa?"

"Yes, I'm okay," she answered. "Don't worry. Finish the exhibition and come back. Stay a few extra days if you want. Enjoy yourself a little."

"Salwa. Stay in the house, *please*. Don't go out. No one knows what's happening."

"Don't be anxious on my account, darling. You enjoy yourself."

Then he said to her for the first time, "I love you."

She was silent and did not reply. She did not tell him that she was in the hospital. It was the first time he had said this to her. She liked *I* more than *love you*. It seemed to have been made especially for her. She heard him smile over the phone. Yes. She had heard him smile, and since that time she had not heard anything from him.

When she tried to save the number he had called from, there was no number. Only the word *Blocked*, in English, on the screen.

When she had first come here, she had tried to call him, but his phone was switched off. She missed him, of course, but she was not worried. She accepted his absences. She did not even think that he should call her in the middle of events like these like any traditional wife. She had convinced herself that they were . . . different.

She thought about him as the music poured into her ears. *Sitting here in limbo / I'm waiting for the toss of the dice*, said the song. The child kicked her, and she smiled a little. Then suddenly she felt something strange in her lower abdomen, followed by an unfamiliar pain.

When the elevator door opened, she found herself in the emergency room. The place was in an uproar, but she heard none of it. People in white and blue clothes rushed right and left while others manned the phones behind the counter. On its own, the song in her ears continued without interruption. She supported herself against a nearby pillar as she bit down on her pain. The stabs of pain increased and became like the waves of Yamm.

Yamm. Yamm. Yamm! The word began to repeat and swell in her head. She focused on her breathing: Inhale, exhale. Inhale, exhale. These words were in the puzzles too, she thought.

Her head filled with strange repeating thoughts, while the song continued to play, indifferent to her mounting pain. *Sitting here in limbo / I have some time to search my soul.* As usual Salwa placed her right hand on her lower belly, as though perhaps to stop the pain, but she did not succeed. The stabs of pain intensified suddenly, and she felt liquid rush out of her. She lifted her gaze for a moment to find a young male doctor standing just like her by the other pillar. He looked at her. She thought that he would come over to ask her what was wrong, but the double doors of the ER split open suddenly and paramedics entered towing a gurney on which a massive man lay unconscious, blood streaming over his face and down his arms. The gurney passed near her and near the young doctor.

As the gurney went past them, Salwa looked at the left arm of the injured man. There was a blue tattoo of a telephone number and address on it. She forgot her pain for a moment and followed the gurney with her eyes as it moved away. The man's face, its features obscured by the quantity of blood, was square. Suspiciously square. Square like a Sudoku puzzle! Then the pain in her belly increased. The stabs were directed lower now. She saw liquid underneath her on the floor tiles. She gave a single scream that brought the young doctor hurrying toward her. Salwa was thinking about the telephone number on the man's arm. She wondered, in the midst of the clamor of her pain, whether the reprinted magazines left behind in her room contained the telephone number for a new publisher's office on the second page, like in the old issues from the eighties. It shocked her that she had not considered this simple detail since putting the magazines on the bedside stand. She began to squeeze the wrist of the young doctor as she closed her eyes, and the song continued in her ears: *Sitting here in limbo / I wait for the stream to flow away / Sitting here in limbo / I know that I must leave.*

At that instant, Salwa became certain that the child was going to come out of her. Now, or in a little while. He would come out.

Her father stood on the sand facing Yamm and holding a bundle of magazines for her. She was looking at him from behind and she knew it was him. She knew also that these were new magazines whose puzzles she had not yet solved. Then the vision transitioned to show the spectral form of her "different" husband. He appeared in front of her, smiling, not laughing. But this time his smile was strange. She sensed that he wanted to explain something to her, but he did not speak. She could almost hear herself cry out to him.

"Where are you, Alfred?"

4

The Events

ILLUS. MOHAMED GABER

HE CALLED THEM "the events."

Rami would say, "The war," and his brother Hassan would correct him: "The events."

Rami's questions never ended. As a child of ten, he had questions about everything. He did not see much of the fighting. He only heard it from behind the wooden shutters covering the windows. Hassan and his mother would move him from room to room whenever the bombing intensified. They would get his bed rolling. Drag it. Rush with it through the hallways of their house in the Caracas neighborhood. From corridor to corridor, from room to room, from the sea-facing side to the interior.

Rami would scream. He would press his palms against his ears. Put his head in his lap. He wished that his legs were stronger. That he could get up from the bed and walk. Run. Fly. His head was filled with hopes, but he could not make any of them come true. He could not even succeed in blocking out the sounds. They increased, they diversified. Hassan brought him cotton to plug his ears, and when the cotton trick stopped working, he gave him a tape recorder with headphones, and after that, other things.

Rami did not know what Hassan did now that he was gone. Did he go into his bedroom? Had he filled up his room with stuff, piled things on his bed?

More than twenty years later, Rami—now in his thirties, his body still small—sat in his wheelchair in front of the lake in the Hamburg public garden and looked out at the clear water. He thought about his big brother, and his mother, who he had found out during his last phone call was beginning to lose her mind. Hassan had put her on the line for him. Rami had asked her, "Mama, how are you?" He heard a deep silence. He felt like he was the only person in the conversation. He tried to provoke her to speak. He said to her, "Mama?" And he choked up. As for her, she did not answer, except to say, "Huh?"

He had kept the call brief. He was confident that his brother was taking care of her just as he had taken care of him when he was young. Rami squeezed the hand of his German girlfriend, who had brought him out of his room to get some fresh air. He studied her delicate fingers for a moment. Then he raised his head and smiled at her tearfully.

With Sophie he had successfully overcome many hurdles, the most important of which were his guilt complex and his self-deprecating questions. When their relationship began to evolve into something romantic, he had asked himself: What makes an attractive girl like her interested in a disabled guy like me? They were not in a film or a TV show. Life was

too complicated for her motivation to be reduced to one of perpetual sacrifice. So why then?

Sophie was firm. "I know," she would say. She knew, and she would deal with the situation. "What's the problem? We'll try it out, and then we'll decide. This is why people don't get married right away. This is why they get to know each other first. This is why they live together."

"But there are obvious issues, Sophie," Rami had replied. "I can't move my legs properly, so how are we supposed to make love? And that's not even considering the other details. We'll do it once, twice, three times, and then what? Will I always be the passive one in our relationship?"

Sophie was insistent that they could overcome all these difficulties, and she was right. In particular he was unable to grasp how she could be so dedicated to going with him to the hospital. How she could be present with him for the physical therapy treatments that never ended, and the exhausting exercises, and the fatigue, and the pain. More than once, when she was in bed with him, he awoke to find her looking at his legs. When he asked her what was the matter, she only smiled and said, "Nothing," and then moved closer to him and held him. It made him feel strange.

He would ask himself, inexperienced as he had been before meeting her: Is this how things work?

Life in Hamburg was easier than in Beirut. Most things were made convenient for people who were disabled or had special needs. Rami went to and from the mechanics laboratory at his university with complete ease. The bus stop was right at the door of the building, and when he returned home the bus dropped him off in front of his apartment, and there was always someone around who would help him. This was the culture here, it seemed.

His apartment had its own story.

When Sophie brought him to see the building for the first time, she pointed out the apartment to him from the outside before they went in. He looked up and said immediately, "We'll take it." She pushed him inside the building, asking him to be patient, at least to inspect the interior first!

Sophie did not know that the shutters of brown wood that covered the windows were enough to make Rami like the building, and then the apartment. At the time she did not know the story.

Ten years, or perhaps more, had passed since his last visit to Beirut, a period during which Rami had never asked himself: Had they kept the same windows in the house in Caracas?

★   ★   ★

I almost cried as I watched the wooden shutters being taken off. They wanted to alter the building's appearance, paint it a new color, put up ugly striped curtains. This was what the committee that managed the building had decided. This was what our neighborhood had come to. It was the era of building committees, and curtains were a fashion that was consuming the balconies of Beirut like a hungry beast extending its reach with no one stopping it. Sometimes I don't understand this country, I thought. How it lurches from one extreme to its opposite. How we create well-organized things inside of things that are not organized inside of things that are organized . . . it's a labyrinth. How each thing is done, and is assimilated, and evolves, and survives. Really, it's a labyrinth.

Sometimes, I don't understand myself.

They closed the narrow street at both ends to prevent cars from entering. I watched the shutters being dropped down from above. The wooden sections made a tremendous noise as they piled up one on top of another, and in doing so produced a cloud of dust that drifted over the group of us standing below. I thought about my brother Rami, and all of the sounds that these shutters had kept out, and the glimpses we had dared to take from time to time between their wooden slats. Were there armed men outside, was the street empty? Was there anyone monitoring the house?

Sometimes, I make justifications for myself.

When did it start? When I put on that dark uniform? Why did I put it on? To protect Rami? When did this really happen? I can't remember. Things get mixed up in my mind. Jump around. Sometimes I recall a memory, think about it, and place it in its correct slot, but then I get anxious. This here is not where it belongs. This thing happened before that one. How does that occur? And why do I make mistakes?

I remember that the guys with guns paid us a visit once. They wanted to inspect the room. They tried to come in, and I prevented them. I told them that my handicapped brother, who was sick, was sleeping inside. They replied that somebody had cursed at them from here. I answered that I would take care of it. One of the young men looked at me suspiciously, but they left.

One day, Layla looked at me, and laid her palm against my cheek, and said that I was no good at expressing myself with my face. She asked me to smile. And when I smiled, she laughed. I asked her what was the matter. She said that this was not a smile, that my real smile was buried deep inside.

Do I really bury my smile? Do I do that on purpose, or not? Or is it my peculiar face that does it? Does my face act in isolation from my mind? Sometimes I feel like I am in one place, and my strange, squarely angled face is in another. Or wait, maybe my facial expressions were what helped me on that night when the guys with guns came?

After their departure, I went into the bedroom. I found Rami in his usual place in the bed, his gaze fixed on the door. I told him that we needed to move the gray parrot to a room that had no windows, or perhaps put it in the foyer. Rami cried. He begged me not to do it. He said that he would stop teaching it insults, and I replied that it was too late for that. He had taught the parrot curse words and that was the end of the discussion, and I was not going to wait for those madmen to

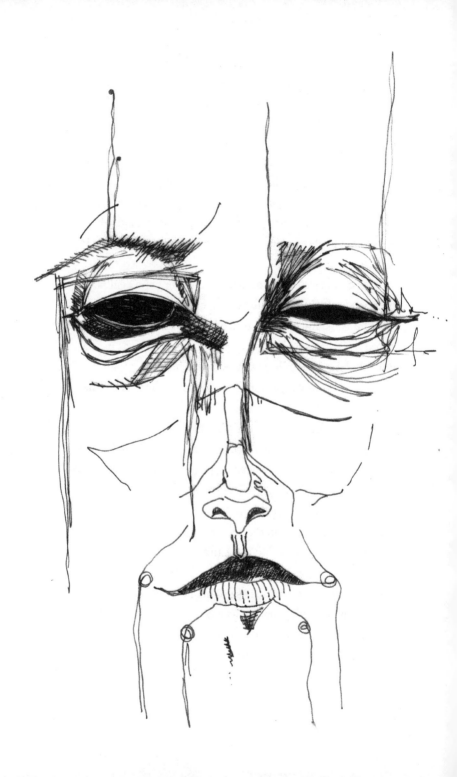

spray the room with bullets from below. They were crazy; they would do it. The oldest of them was not more than twenty. Rami began to cry hysterically. How old was he? Ten? He cried and I promised him that I would get him a rolling chair so he would be able to move around more in the house. He looked at me and continued crying. Was my face somewhere else?

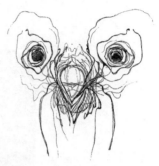

Was this what made him continue to cry?

★ ★ ★

In the darkness, Sophie stood before the window and looked at Rami sleeping in the bed, and she smiled a ghost of a smile. She cried, careful not to make any sound. She did not know why she was crying. She felt only that she must cry. She looked out through the shutters, and the view appeared to her segmented by the wooden slats. She had never understood why Rami kept the shutters closed when he was in the room. When he was at the university, she would seize the opportunity to open all the windows. To expose the apartment to the air. She would try to get rid of the stale air from inside. If Rami had thought about it in a logical manner, he would have asked her to do that. Stale air in particular was not good for him. But when it came to this detail, he said "No" in an oddly decisive way.

It was an eerie sort of night. From outside came the sound of cats mewing. Is it mating season? she wondered. No. So why are the animals making those noises? Such questions passed through Sophie's head and she could find no answers to them. She thought about the members of her family who had never

left their distant farm, and about all the animals that she used to live among there. She felt a profound sadness that was difficult for her to describe. As if the sadness were a deep well, and when she reached her hand inside it there was nothing there, and then her hand floated to the surface and collided with the wooden side that was just like this window shutter. But here, unlike if she had been in the well, she could see what was happening outside, even though the view was incomplete. Here is the baker in the opposite building opening the sliding door of his shop, she thought, and here is a garbage truck driving by and stopping next to the trash bin, and here is a young boy running through the dark square and passing both the shop and the truck.

In her segmented view, the boy's legs appeared. They passed from the right side of her line of sight to the left before they disappeared. At once Sophie turned to Rami in the bed. She stared at his legs under the blankets, and she felt her sadness sink further into the depths of the well and stay there.

She walked toward the bed, holding back her tears with the pressure of her hands. She climbed into the bed carefully. Rami was sleeping with his mouth open. His cheek twitched slightly. This was a motion he made often while sleeping. This was not the first time Sophie had noticed it.

She kept looking at Rami, trying not to think about her sadness. She would not let her thoughts progress in that direction. Because she wanted to fill her head with other thoughts, and there was nothing but Rami's face in front of her to inspire her, she continued watching him. That muscle in Rami's cheek twitched again. She wondered, Is this twitch a product of what he's seeing in his dream?

Is he dreaming right now?

127

* * *

Who did Rami visit in his sleep?

He was flying. He could see the tips of buildings piercing through the dark clouds. His legs moved fluidly. They flapped in the air. He began to descend toward the rooftops. The air rushed past his skin. When he looked up, he found that the clouds were now above him. Their insides were white. Now he was between the buildings. As he passed balconies and windows, he kicked in the air. He grabbed onto the railing of one of the balconies, and he tried to look through the window. All of the shutters on the buildings were closed. As if they were declining to disclose what was within them. As if they were collaborating to conceal anything that would affirm the identity of this place. But Rami knew that he was in Beirut. He tried to concentrate and remember the reasons that had led him to such absolute certainty, but he could not marshal his thoughts. He continued his flight from one balcony to another, hoping he would find something different, and when he did not, he landed on the ground. The tar on the street was new. No pits, no potholes, no debris. He looked at his legs first, and then he moved his right leg forward and it responded. He moved his left leg forward, and it responded too. Soon he found himself walking like any normal person. The street was utterly empty. No one was out. The shops were closed. He observed that they all had sliding iron doors just as they had in the eighties.

Was he in another time?

He started walking again, and then he began to jog. The road in front of him lengthened and curved, then straightened out, then twisted again. The number of adjoining buildings surrounding him on either side did not diminish. Although their colors and shapes began to vary as he went on, they still appeared alike to him. There was only the one street. It did not end and it did not intersect with other streets. He saw himself from behind as he walked. He saw himself running. He was advancing further into the image. As if someone were coiling a spring somewhere and making him hurry onward. As he ran, he lifted his eyes again to the clouds and thought that he could not understand this.

He would never understand this.

★   ★   ★

Sophie woke up in the early morning, before Rami. How long had she slept? She did not look at the clock and so did not find out. She felt weak, but sleep had escaped her. She remained in bed for a little while, looking at the ceiling. It was blank. She thought that she could fill it with drawings, but then she rejected the idea. Someone was doing this very thing right now somewhere else in the world, she thought.

She got lightly out of bed, picked up her clothes from outside the closet, and went out of the room. She closed the door behind her and proceeded to dress in the entryway. Then she descended the stairs quietly to her bicycle, which was parked in the lobby of the building.

Sophie rode for a long time. Perhaps nearly an hour. She passed the closer train station and kept going until she reached another one, further away and larger. In the plaza in front of the station, she stood for a moment by her bike and looked at the massive building and at all of those legs entering and exiting through the doors. She approached and entered the main lobby. She headed quickly toward the line at the ticket window. Then she stopped. The people in here were all moving slowly. She kept her eyes fixed on the ground and stepped forward automatically whenever she found an empty space created in front of her. When she reached the window, the man selling tickets asked her for her destination and which train she wanted to book. She was silent, so the ticket-seller asked again. She found herself apologizing to him and leaving the line. She hurried outside again, without looking behind her. She paused again at her bicycle. Suddenly, a bus passed by in the street and stopped nearby. Sophie unlocked her bicycle, got on, and rode quickly toward it. Then she dismounted, picked up the bike, and boarded the bus.

★   ★   ★

How do events repeat themselves? Do things happen for a purpose? Is there someone out there who can send me a sign?

I asked myself these questions when I found myself again facing the same scene. A violent knock at the door, and then boys appear carrying weapons, the oldest of them not yet twenty. One of them says to me, "Abu Ahmad is asking about you," so I go with them, after instructing our neighbor to stay with Mama.

It is the same scene with only slight differences: the clothes, for example. These are not 1980s clothes. The sleeves back then were looser, and they extended from the shoulder to the elbow. Clothing these days reveals more of the shoulder. The bodies of today's youths have begun their assault on these tight clothes — the former seem to be encroaching on the latter, and not the reverse.

But the weapons are the same. They are old. I know them. I remember them. From which plots of earth did they dig these up? I buried my weapons in the back garden of our country house, and I permitted no one to till the ground there. Mama was even forbidden from growing seedlings for parsley and tomatoes and potatoes. Potatoes were what kept me up at night most, for they grow beneath the earth. I imagined a scene in which Mama would bend down one summer to pull up the stem of a potato plant, and up with it would come the muzzle of a gun. This does not only happen in films. Films have stolen a lot from what happened here in the eighties, even if some of the details were modified when they were put on the screen.

I would take Rami in the wheelchair and go with him to Cinéma Strand. It was there we watched the film *Christopher Columbus*, and it was there Rami saw his first pair of breasts onscreen — they belonged to one of the Indian girls Christopher met after disembarking from his ship.

These were normal things to learn from the movies. Their effect on me, however, was different. Something inside of me was touched whenever I found myself faced with one of those opening sequences where music is overlaid with the voice of a man: talking to us about the regular day ahead of him, or about his first day of school, or about the day he met his true love or his mother died, or perhaps about the day on which the event occurred that will be the pivot point for everything that happens in the film, or about the last day of his life.

The camera starts from above and everything we see looks far away, spread out, miniature, and then it plunges with us over the first cloud, and then the second, and we rush closer first to see the city from overhead, then the roofs of the buildings, then the streets, until we enter through a window into a room, and through a door to a staircase, and from floor to floor into corridors to other rooms. The voice does not stop speaking to us in words contrived to pull us into the story. Then I am lost. I am now inside the image on the screen, and I begin to talk to myself and narrate my own story.

But where do I start my story? How do we pick the moments at which our stories begin?

★   ★   ★

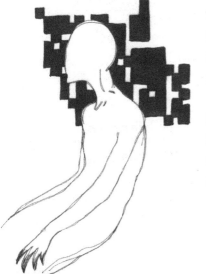

The main issue is to understand how the axes of movement and the surfaces on which the thing moves are designed.

In the university lab, Rami sat looking at the model he had made. He tried engaging the metal arm suspended above it on a clamp. The model moved in the direction he wanted. He experimented with bending it further. He found that the arm stopped at a certain angle. He measured it, and looked again at his drawings on the sheet of paper, and wrote down the measurement of the angle. He moved closer in his wheelchair to the computer screen and studied the digital plans that his colleagues in the department had prepared, and he decided that he needed to increase the angle to enable the arm to bend more when the electronic command was sent.

After he recorded his notes, he looked at his cell phone. Its screen was quiet. There was no call from Sophie. He checked the text messages. Nothing. He looked at the clock and found that he had spent close to four hours in the lab. This was strange. Where was Sophie? Hadn't they agreed to see a film tonight?

He picked up his phone and called her.

★ ★ ★

Sophie bought a breadstick at the kiosk in the middle of the park. Then she walked her bicycle toward the lake. There were not many other people there. She could have counted on one hand the few who were walking or sitting in her vicinity. At the lake, she parked her bike, sat down on a stone bench, and began to divide up the breadstick and toss the crumbled pieces into the water. The ducks vied with one another to get closer. Sophie kept throwing the bread until she was down to half the stick. Then she began to break off pieces of it and eat them. She felt suddenly hungry. She remembered that she had not eaten anything since the morning. Maybe the sleeplessness of the previous night was what made her feel so drained. Her arms and legs were tired from biking. She stood up and flung what was left of the breadstick into the lake, and then she began to walk her bike along the forking path among the vegetation.

She heard her phone ring from inside her purse in the basket of the bike, but she continued on her way and did not take it out. The ringing went on and on. The ringtone ended and started again. Sophie quickened her steps. When she stopped for a moment and the phone ceased to ring, her eyes overflowed with tears. She looked around and there was no one there, so she did not try to suppress her sobs.

★   ★   ★

I feel like my life in Lebanon has always been full of repeated attempts to avoid things. I avoid pain, I avoid injury. I avoid the worst for what is only bad. There you have it. I avoid the worst for what is bad. That's it. I can even add to this and say that I have avoided what is bad too, if it might hurt me or my family, by harming another person. Sometimes this works in our own minds. Not in reality. It works the moment you think about it, if you are living in the moment. It makes us feel better. And what about me? Maybe I needed an excuse? The first time, I joined up with them to protect Rami. I secured the street. I prevented any shooting from taking place there. Anything that might turn into a problem, I drove it far from our house. But Caracas is on a slope abutting the sea, and it was not possible to ward off what spilled over into the streets from the sea. The same thing applied to the sky. I could not keep it away from us. I controlled only a small territory.

But what happened this time? Did I want to protect Mama? I do not have to fight. From the beginning we realized that this would be a localized war. And from the beginning I knew that no one would bother us in Hamra. Why did I go, then, to Abu Ahmad? Did something tell me I had to do this? Did I want to see what was happening? I know that whenever I walked down the street, I could see the differences. In the last war, there were solid reasons for many of those who took part. Now, what are the reasons? I do not understand, in spite of all the explanations offered on TV, speeches that contradict each other. A hundred reasons are given. Except for that period in the past during which we used to live without living, there is nothing driving this explosion. All the talk is unconvincing. It's useless, as useless as trying to summarize in a few words the issue between us and them, or even just our side of it.

As for the veterans among us, we who secured the streets last time, our faces looked extraordinarily ancient. Even our bodies appeared strangely too big, as if having made it through all these years they refused now to conform to the new clothes. I recognized more than one face. Some of them had been on the other side in the last war. Some of us had shot at each other. And now we laughed, and clinked glasses of arak, and stuffed mortadella between slices of French bread, and popped cans of sardines.

As I devoured a sandwich, I looked at the other men around me. They were laughing. I enjoyed a voiceover moment, like in the films at Cinéma Strand. I began to ask: Where did they come from? Did the cell doors open for them? Or are they like me, living in apartments, taking care of their sick mothers, doling out satellite TV cables to the other residents on their streets?

And then: Isn't the story spoiled when it's cut short?

Rami sat alone in the movie theater. He had chosen a film no one else was watching. He was in the last row, in his wheelchair. His cell phone was in his lap, and he looked at it from time to time to check whether he had received a call or text message from Sophie. When he gave up looking, he began to pay attention to the film for the first time. It was an old silent film that imposed no sound on the viewer except its music. The actors hurried past, moving with slightly more speed than necessary and with more extreme facial expressions. Was this how the past had been? thought Rami. Faster? More obvious? He was not a fan of bestowing positive adjectives exclusively upon what was past. He remembered the days of the war in Beirut. They were not beautiful or good in the least, for example. So was he bestowing the adjectives of his crisis upon this film instead? Was movement the issue? Was it his legs? He would not find answers to his questions. They were of the sort that only circled endlessly through his head. They might affect his actions, but they did not come with answers. It was in their essence not to have answers. It was in their essence that they pushed him onward. That they walked him down a certain route. Yet he would never be able to walk on his own. He would stay sitting in this chair. Whenever somebody abandoned him, the questions attacked him. They besieged him, they finished him off.

He tried to escape the exaggerated movement in the film by looking at the walls of the theater itself. It reminded him of that cinema in Hamra. What was its name? Did they reopen it? During his last visit to Lebanon, Hassan had taken him for a walk in his wheelchair on Hamra Street. They passed the theater.

There were signs posted behind the cinema's glass doors, which were padlocked with chains: "Opening Soon." He went by there more than once during his stay in Beirut. He continued to see: "Opening." He continued to see: "Soon."

He remembered the cinema's seats but had forgotten its name. They were just like these seats. He remembered the high ceiling. Just like the one here. As if something about this height suited the stale movies within. He remembered the stench of humidity during the last film he saw there before they closed the theater. He thought about the fetid odor until it almost entered his nose again, but he was unable to remember the film itself, and he did not know why.

He missed Hassan suddenly. He would call him when he returned home. He had called him every day since the outbreak of the crisis in Beirut. Hassan never answered right away but always called him back later. He would say that he had been in the bathroom, or sleeping, or taking care of Mama. Yesterday it occurred to Rami that Hassan might be hiding something from him. Was Mama sick? Had something happened? More than one possibility crossed his mind, but he buried all of it the moment his brother returned his call.

Rami picked up his phone and began to reread the old messages on it. The film on the screen was ending. The whole film had gone by and Sophie had not called him.

★ ★ ★

Sophie lay down on the bed in the hotel room. She reached her hand into her bag, and after a few moments of searching, she withdrew a slip of paper.

She sat up on the edge of the bed and opened the folded paper to reveal the Lebanese telephone number written on it. It was the very same number. It had never changed. Why hadn't she saved it in the memory of her phone, since she used it so often? She was unable to do that. She had tried and failed. More than once she had saved it, then erased it. She felt no desire to have it in her cell phone. She let it remain scribbled on a scrap of paper, and she would transfer it from bag to bag, and from drawer to drawer, keeping it away from Rami. The piece of paper grew tattered as time passed, until she was obliged at one point to copy the number onto a new one and throw the old one away.

Sophie lifted the receiver of the hotel room phone and dialed the number. She waited through several seconds of complete silence before she heard the voice of the Lebanese operator telling her that the number was not available. She returned the receiver to its place, and she looked down at the floor of the room, which was covered in thick carpet. She thought about Rami. How had he gotten up the stairs to the apartment today? Had he been able to manage? She thought about returning but quickly banished the idea in a flood of tears. Her legs were pressed together and her elbows propped against them while her palms covered her face. The tears soaked her hands, and she was unable to stop them. This was the first time she had cried like this in a while. Everything seemed to inflate and grow bigger. Her memory took her back to that mysterious phone call she had received two years ago. As she sat there with her eyes closed, the images assaulted her. She took away her wet hands, opened her eyes, and released some of the tension she felt in a loud sob. From her hands, a single teardrop fell and disappeared unseen into the dark brown carpet.

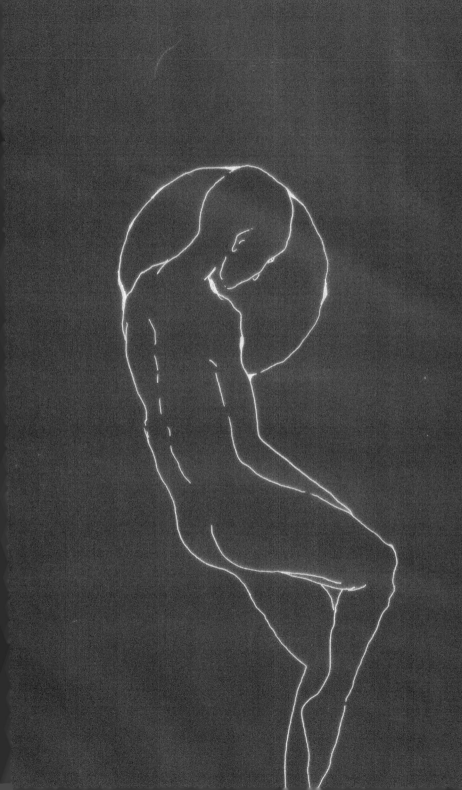

★ ★ ★

In Rami's dream, the single street did not continue infinitely. As he jogged, he found that the buildings around him were sinking into the ground.

They were plunging into the asphalt, whole, without a sound. As if, as they sank, they were following a course to which they were already accustomed. Rami stopped and looked down at half of a window showing above the street, and then before he could make out the interior of the apartment through it, the entire window vanished underground. He watched the window above follow it down. He moved away and kept walking as he looked around at what was happening. In front of him another scene was unfolding. Suddenly he understood what was going on. The entire city was sinking and its subterranean level was rising from underneath it. An older version of it was being raised. The buildings were different, the stones different, the sidewalks different. The asphalt alone remained as it was. Scarcely had Rami noted this detail when he saw a crack appearing in the middle of the road. It was heading his way, but he did not feel that he should be afraid. He was sure that the crack would wait for him to move out of the way. Given this certainty, he took his time getting closer to the buildings, and what he had expected happened. The fissure stopped advancing just before it reached him. Rami placed his hands on the marble railing of a balcony on one of the new buildings and scaled it. As soon as he had made it onto the balcony, the fissure began to move again, continuing its progress down the middle of the street. Then it began to widen, without affecting the new buildings on both sides of the road, to expose underneath it another strip of asphalt. The old asphalt slid down the sides and disappeared. Before long the whole street had changed its skin, making Rami think that now he must be entering a different film.

★ ★ ★

When Abu Ahmad spoke to me, he said a lot of contradictory things. First of all, I did not understand why they had brought me to him, and second, I did not understand why me in particular. But I had been invited. They gave me a little money, and they said that they would give me more when things became clearer.

I did not talk. I only listened. Then I returned to the house. I looked in on Mama sleeping, and then I went out again and knocked on our neighbor's door. I asked her to look after Mama for the next two days, and I gave her the money I had gotten from them.

Hamra was strange that evening, as if it were preparing itself for something. The streets began to empty of people at four o'clock. The crowds disappeared. I had taken to carrying my ID card and my papers at all times, in the back pocket of my pants. I took out my cell phone as I walked and scrolled through the numbers until I found the one I wanted, and I dialed it. The phone rang five times before a female voice came on speaking English in a German accent, and I responded in my own poor English, "Hello."

"Hello. I cannot speak just now."

"He is near from you?"

"In the other room."

"Okay. I am not going to talk so much. Listen. Maybe something happens to me. If it does, I want you to take care of him."

141

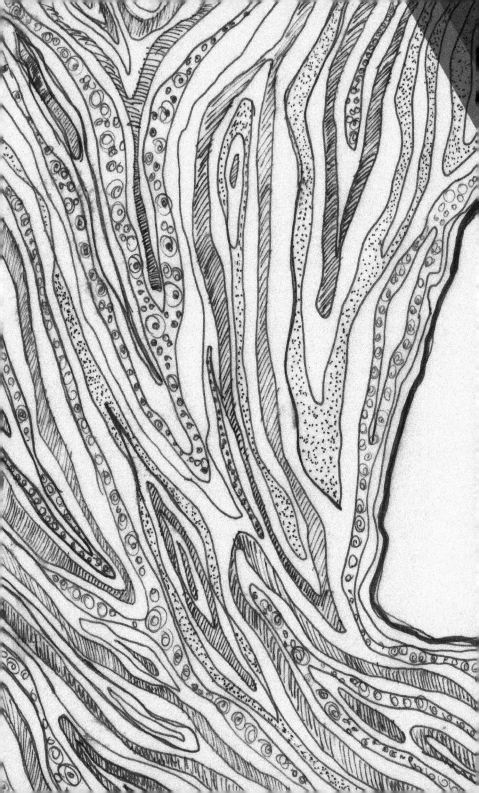

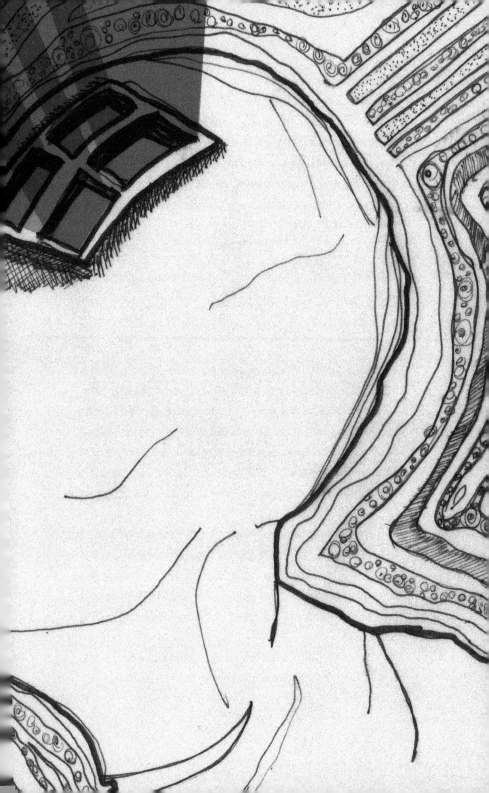

"I do not understand."

"It is not possible for me . . ."

"Listen to me, I'll ring you soon. He's calling for me."

I sighed once. I sighed many times. Alone on the street, I began to inhale deeply. I filled my lungs with air. I felt the pressure in my ears and chest. As I walked, I noticed a glass display window crammed full of strange objects. A printout in English was fixed to the glass:

"Tattoos"

I did not pause long before the window. I pushed open the door and went in.

★   ★   ★

In the hotel garden, Sophie stared at the dark screen of her cell phone. She put her finger to the power button, but then she changed her mind and threw the device back into her bag. She focused her gaze on her plate of breakfast. Beyond the edge of the plate, she noticed a small boy playing by the chair of a woman who appeared to be his mother. He was very near, and she imagined that she saw him smile suddenly and wave his fingers at her.

The boy reminded her of her sister's children. He reminded her of that phase in her life when she used to see her family once a month. She would come to the house in the country, bearing fruits from the city and red wine for her father. When he said to her, "We have lots of wine here," she would reply, "This wine is imported."

The boy made her remember those days when her mother would ask her about her work and she would reply that

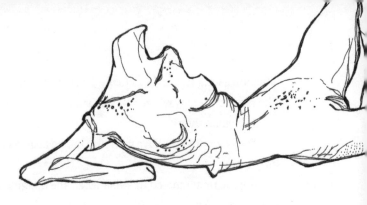

everything was fine at the university. He made her remember her
lie—when in fact she was selling sex to every young man at the
club who wanted her. She would talk herself into it by telling herself: This is not a whorehouse. This is a gentlemen's club. She
would tell herself: I'm not here all the time. I am asked to come
here. I come twice a week. I do what I want during the day. Here
the customers are different, and things are nicer. Here everything
is carefully defined from the beginning, and the customers are
who they are. The same faces were repeated so often that she and
the other girls saw a new one only every few months.

Until that Lebanese man visited the club. They called her
in and told her that this was a new customer. The Lebanese pay
well. She entered the room. She waited for him to get things
started. But he sat down on the couch and said in English, "I
have a friend who needs . . ." Then he stopped and rearranged
his words. "My friend, he has a brother here in Germany, not too
far from this place. My friend will give you money every month.
It will be a full-time job."

"What's the job?"

"His brother . . . he does not walk."

"He needs a nurse?"

"No. He doesn't need so much care. He became used to his

situation a long time ago. Actually, he studies at the university. The same university where you also study."

"So what, then?"

"Get close to him. Live with him in one apartment. Make love to him."

Sophie remembered this visit when she imagined that she saw the young boy smile.

★ ★ ★

The new asphalt was hot. Rami stepped onto it and felt the heat rising into his body from his feet. He began to run again. This time he found himself in the middle of a wide square with seven gates around it. He jumped onto a nearby balcony and took off his shoes. Their soles had melted from the heat of the ground. He walked around on the flagstones until the bottoms of his feet felt cool again. Then he stopped and surveyed the square with its many gates. There was no one out there except for two turbaned men wearing identical cloaks. The men were marching together from gate to gate and stopping at each one so the first man could ask the second, "Here?"

"No. The story says he will come from the west. From the sea."

They walked to another gate some distance from the beach and repeated the same dialogue. Rami could hear them as perfectly as if they were sitting next to him on the balcony. It was strange and illogical for the sound to reach him here, and he did not understand it. He also did not understand why the two men had to repeat the same dialogue in front of every gate, even those that didn't face west.

After five or six gates (Rami lost count), the first man halted and said to his companion, "Two gates are left: Bab El Santiyeh and Bab Idris."

The other replied, "Let's split up."

Rami watched the men as they went off in different directions. One of them stood in front of Bab El Santiyeh, and the other stood in front of Bab Idris. The distance between the two men shrank. Rami thought that this made sense because it was a dream. He was moving without caring whether he made noise. He knew that they could not sense his presence, and that although he could see them, they could not see him.

He relocated to another balcony facing the beach, and from there what was beyond the two gates became visible. The two men raised their staffs in the air as though bracing for something. Rami could make out precisely what was approaching from beyond the gates: a monstrous wave, racing toward the beach. He saw it advance on the two men. Suddenly, a green body appeared in the water. Something long. A tail. The tail lifted into the air and slapped the crest of the wave, without breaking it. The wave's size and the speed of its forward progress did not change. A soft breeze brushed Rami's skin. Then the breeze gathered strength. It became a gust, then a wind, then a gale, and he felt the sea spray on his face. He gripped the edge of the balcony, though he was not afraid and did not flee.

The two men were ready.

He heard a powerful voice that he could not describe even in the dream.

A voice that resembled . . .

★ ★ ★

The situation deteriorated, and it became necessary for me to protect myself. I wanted to prove to them that I had not come to infiltrate their group. What a confusing life this is. They sent for me because they wanted me in a battle, and then when they realized that I was using only the minimum number of bullets and taking care not to aim at anyone, they doubted me. Was it I who had come here originally? Weren't they the ones who had brought me?

Stupid teenagers! They stood in corners, behind walls, and opened fire at random. They all knew each other. They even knew the names of each other's sisters and mothers. They exchanged taunts before and after firing off each clip of bullets. They said: *This is for your sister! Put this up your mama's ass!* I saw them doing it.

Stupid.

But hadn't the war been like this too? Maybe it was just that I had changed? No. No. The war was different. The war was longer, smellier, more violent. I was deep inside the war. No. It was inside me. Here, what am I doing? What is this? Am I with them or not with them? Aren't they correct to doubt me, then? Why did I come anyway?

Hajj Ahmad was standing talking with them in the courtyard in front of the Crowne Plaza Hotel. I waited nearby until he finished with his instructions and his reprimands. I looked at the number and address I'd had tattooed on my arm. The skin was inflamed. Maybe the idiot tattoo artist hadn't known how to do it properly, or maybe he didn't sterilize the tools. He had looked at me when I came into the shop as if seeing a ghost, and he had appeared almost embarrassed, as though he'd been doing something illicit and I had interrupted him in the act. I explained to him what I wanted tattooed, and I handed him the piece of paper with the number on it. He stared at it for a second and then he asked me to follow him inside where the procedure would be done. There, he began to show me other designs, saying that he could tattoo them in a frame around the number. I replied that I wanted neither frames nor ornaments. Just the number. The young fellow went on tirelessly trying to convince me, until my patience wore thin and I found myself shouting at him as I had never shouted at anyone before. His persistence succeeded in bringing me to this state. For my part, I was under a lot of pressure.

I felt the importance of what I was doing. I had never tattooed my body before. This was my first try. I was not doing it to get attention—otherwise, I would have chosen one of the designs that the young man showed me, something more attractive than a telephone number and address written the length of my arm.

"Why are you here?"

Abu Ahmad's question interrupted my recollections. He looked at me, then at my arm, and he regarded me with a look whose meaning I did not understand.

"You sent for me, Abu . . . ," I began, but Abu Ahmad cut me off before I finished my sentence.

"No . . . you know what I mean. You're here. Why? The boys

told me that while they were fighting, you were standing back watching." He sighed, then he continued, "Hassan . . . go back home. You don't have to stay if you don't want to. But I can't guarantee to you what these boys will do next. From now on they'll be in charge of the neighborhood."

"Am I doing something I shouldn't be?"

Abu Ahmad laughed. "The issue isn't what you're doing, it's what you're not. You can't just sit there swatting flies all day. I know you, but these guys are unpredictable. Imagine for example that a rumor starts going around that you were spying on them."

"Spying?"

"Yes! Spying! Where do you think you are?"

I looked at Abu Ahmad and nodded, indicating that I would behave. He went to lead some of the young men in prayer on the sidewalk in front of the hotel courtyard, and I walked away. I passed by some of the other guys standing on a corner close by, drinking beer and smoking what remained in their packs of cigarettes. I stood with them and one of them gave me a cigarette. They were arguing about tonight's battle.

★   ★   ★

A knock on the door of Sophie's room. She stood up and opened it. A young man in workout clothes stepped inside, inspecting the small room as he entered. Sophie closed the door and followed him. She got to the curtains before he did and drew them closed with a single tug of her hand, plunging the room into midday darkness. Then she paused and turned to the young man, who threw down his bag and began to take off his shoes.

"Wait."

Looking at her now, he removed the second shoe more slowly, showing her that he was waiting to hear what she would say next.

"I don't want to do this."

The young man began to speak irritably in German. It was clear from his accent that he was not from Hamburg. "But you called the club and said you wanted me. I postponed another appointment for this!"

"Don't worry, I'll pay you whatever amount was agreed on. But first I'd like to talk."

The young man looked at her uncomprehendingly. "This is a waste of time. I can't . . ."

"Don't be afraid. I just want to speak with you. Don't worry, I'm not crazy or mentally disturbed or anything."

The man looked at her with the same irritated expression and said, "I'm not afraid. What do you want to know?"

"How do you feel when you sleep with a woman for money?"

"I expected this question."

"Well?"

"I don't feel only one thing. It depends on the person. Sometimes I like it. Sometimes I feel something. At other times it's just a job."

"Do you feel guilty?"

The young man looked Sophie directly in the eyes and demanded, "Why are you asking? What about you, do you feel guilty?"

★   ★   ★

If only I could tell my story like the voice at the beginnings of the films I used to watch at Cinéma Strand. Accompany my actions in the film with anticipation-inducing sentences of this type:

I love coffee. I make it every day. I bring it to a boil four times on the stove, at seven in the morning. But today I did not sleep at home. I did not drink coffee. I woke up two hours before seven. Today everything was different. And tomorrow will be more different still. How? I do not yet know the details. I am still discovering them myself.

But nothing is this easy. If only I was really granted this moment. If only I was able to see myself from the outside. To study aspects of myself I had not noticed before. If only.

That morning, I left the party headquarters. All the younger guys were sleeping. I thought about what Abu Ahmad had said to me. Before I started off, I removed the bandage from my tattoo and looked at it. The entire thing was swollen, glowing as if it wanted to tell me something.

I walked through Hamra, yawning. I carried my weapon over my shoulder. For the first time, it felt heavy to me. I patrolled the area in never-ending circuits. I would come out of a side street perpendicular to Hamra Street, walk a little ways down the street, and then enter another cross street and repeat the whole thing again. I kept lengthening the distances I was covering, and searching, and finding nothing.

I talked to myself. I remembered saying good-bye to Rami in the airport years earlier. How much time had passed since then? I felt like this had happened a very long time ago, yet despite this it seemed to me that time was racing by, as if he had departed only yesterday.

When he brought me the sheet of paper showing he'd been admitted to the university, I was glad, though I did not say so outright. He would not remain a prisoner of his room. He would not be harassed whenever he went out as had happened to him here for years. Here they did not understand. Here they pitied him. It was hard on Rami. He couldn't bear it any longer. But along with his excitement at the letter of admission, he felt guilty. He started to talk to me about Mama. As I listened to him, silence overcame me. I was lost in another world. Then I returned to the present and declared that I was happy for him. I told him, "Go."

He looked at me as if to make sure he had heard right, so I repeated the command I had given. "Go. When are you supposed to be there?"

And so Rami left, and our communication became limited to phone calls. But with the passing of time, I began to feel that something was not right. One time I asked him jokingly, "How's your love life there?"

"Who could love someone like me?" His tone was self-mocking.

His words did not surprise me. I had been expecting them from him some day. But they also took me back years, to a chair in a seaside café where I sat facing Layla. I had used the same phrase with her. I'd asked her, "How can someone like you love someone like me?"

Layla smiled and did not answer, and then she asked me to stop being

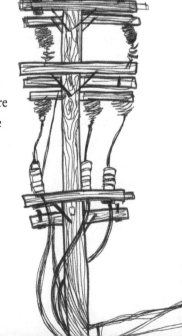

154

stupid. This happened before she was kidnapped and disappeared. I never did find her. A short time after Rami's departure,
I went to the press syndicate and stood in a room filled with
other people who had lost someone to kidnapping. I scoured the
photos taped to the chairs for a picture of Layla. Had someone
put her here? Was someone pursuing her case? I considered,
without being afraid, that one of those present might recognize
me as a former member of a militia. But I had never kidnapped
anyone. I used to say that kidnapping was one thing, and killing
was something else. During the clashes you never know who
you have killed, even if you walk past the corpses afterward.
You will not know that it was you who transformed this living
person into a corpse. The matter is always open to doubt. As for
the man you kidnap, he is right there in front of you. You see his
face, and when you finally do away with him you will have killed
a face that you actually saw. I used to say that I only defended
and protected, and that everything else I was forced into.

As my eyes searched for a picture of Layla on the chairs, I
resolved to protect Rami. I said to myself that I would bring him
love, and I did.

These scenes passed before me as I walked in the dawn
hours of that day. I saw them play out on the uneven paving
stones of Hamra Street. I continued to be burdened by the
weight of my weapon, which seemed to increase with every step,
until I reached the end of the street. There I found a young man
drawing on the wall. I knew him. I had seen him on our street
more than once. And there, the idea again overpowered me. I
will protect myself this time. I will not kidnap him. I will not
harm him. I will just bring the boy to Abu Ahmad. I will prove
my loyalty with this act. Anyway, I am protecting the young man

by getting him away from here. No one knows what could happen if one of those idiots saw him.

I stood pointing my weapon in his direction, and I uttered two or three sentences. I don't remember what I said. Strange that I do not remember. The young man did not speak. He looked at me and at his equipment, and he did not speak.

What happened after that?

Everything happened in a rush, though I was unaware of it. I knew that I had died only when I discovered that I possessed language. I became certain of my death when I found my own voice. This voice.

★　★　★

Before he could learn whether the wave had drowned the brand-new city, a shout from the street woke him. For the first few seconds that followed his awakening, Rami was unable to recall his dream. He knew that he had dreamed, and that he might remember some of it later, as he usually did. But this time he was anxious to recall what he had seen as quickly as possible. He was sure that he had not seen a complete dream. He almost asked himself: Can dreams be completed?

He banished these thoughts, and as he prepared his coffee at the stove, he smiled. He remembered that today he was going with Sophie to the cinema. He thought, then, that everything would be all right.

Today, and tomorrow, and the day after.

5 *The Decisive Moment*

ILLUS. MOHAMED GABER

This is a love story that has never yet been told.

Pause

Sanaa, this is how I see our story. I have not told it to you, neither have you told it to me. The story, with all its particularities, simply ebbed away and we did not stop to ask what had happened. We did not press the PAUSE button, for example, and go back to look. We did not step away from the picture so we could question our actions. Was this our critical error? I search for an excuse, for a reason, and I cannot find one. Shouldn't there be a clear reason for what happened? Should there be? Should there be, or is this only what I wish? Does a clear reason make everything else clearer and easier? Or does it make things more difficult? Is there a difference? Is there anyone who actually craves difficulty and ambiguity? Perhaps. But I, certainly, am not one of those people, nor do we know anyone like that, and I think you agree with me here.

I say *I think*, because we broke up. The period after a breakup—*I think*—can no longer abide assurances. And anyway, if certainty were so certain, would the breakup have happened?

Is it all so scientifically simple? I don't know. Maybe all things come with certain difficulties and it's just that I'm being stubborn?

After our breakup, I fought meaningless battles with my mother and father. I had only a few friends left, and even many of these I hadn't seen in a long time. I realized that I had, when we were together, isolated myself from the world. When we split up, the friends we still had felt uncomfortable. Who should they stay in touch with? You or me? In the beginning they would see both of us separately, but later on, I think, they started to feel weird about it, just like I did. To spare them the awkwardness, I asked them to see you whenever they could and told them not to invite me when they got together if you would be there.

We wanted to be "civilized" when we parted ways. You hoped we could still talk. You apologized for your choice of phrase, steeped as it was in cliché: "Let's stay friends." Then you clarified: "Not like we are now." You said that you truly did not want us to stop talking. That you were just taking the pressure off our relationship.

I asked you to give me one day. "Twenty-four hours," I said. You looked at me and said that you understood what I meant. But when I realized what you thought, I hastened to assure you that I wouldn't run away. "Just twenty-four hours, then we'll see."

When we met again, I didn't tell you what I had done during those twenty-four hours, for in a period of separation, although we may talk, we don't feel ourselves compelled to share everything. During a separation the omissions begin, and riddles left unsolved and unfinished become normal. Interest and disinterest alike become natural.

That was my first false step.

24 Hours

"The view is good from up there."

I said this to you the first time we climbed up on the roof of a building. That was in my first apartment, in Zokak El Blat, before I moved to Hamra.

Step by step we ascended the staircase, and to our good fortune, the door to the roof was open. There, we found cages of pigeons. The birds rose up suddenly and shook themselves when we pushed open the door. They soared into the sky as though launched from a propeller, and then they landed again beside their wooden homes. You approached them and they didn't try to escape. You picked one up and showed it to me. You said that its eyes were jealous.

Although climbing onto the roofs of the buildings in Ras Beirut became a tradition of ours, I continued to remember our first climb. How we stood looking into the distance, as between us prevailed a silence interrupted only by the strange cry of the pigeons. This period of silence was repeated after every one of our quarrels over trivial things, making me believe that when we disagreed we were only looking into the distance. But were we seeing different things? Were we approaching that decisive moment when you asked for things between us to end? Or were we simply seeing what was in front of us, without applying ourselves to the existential questions that I believed a silence like this required?

We would stand together at the moment of sunset and abandon our eyes to the vastness of the scene. How many sunsets did we watch together, Sanaa? Why do I remember these details, when I don't have an answer? *The mind behaves strangely.* These are your words. You spoke them once.

During the twenty-four hours I requested from you, I saw more than one sunset. I climbed up and down adjoining buildings on that sloping street in the Caracas neighborhood. I went up in a rush and I came down in a rush. I didn't notice my clothes sticking to me from the sweat flowing from every pore on my body. I didn't even feel myself gasping for air. I would pause on the rooftop, watch the sunset for an instant, then descend and hurry on to a new building, a new rooftop.

Each rooftop made me see a different sunset. No, the rooftop did not make me see. I saw. It was I who deluded myself into thinking that I saw.

During those twenty-four hours, I wore myself out looking into the distance. I was trying to understand where we had diverged, and I couldn't. But before long these thoughts of mine gave way to hysterical action. Climbing the stairs and descending the stairs, until the sun vanished and the sky went black. Only then did I stretch out full-length on top of one of the roofs, whose location I no longer remember—which seems odd to me—and look at the stars.

I could hear myself panting as I never had before, and it seemed to me that my heartbeats were growing louder, and that

I was dying. Then I told myself that this was not the sound of my heart alone but that of the stars addressing me in my time of loss, and that perhaps I should let myself drift off to sleep to allow them to speak to me.

In the few moments before I fell asleep looking at the sky, I decided to start a correspondence with you, Sanaa. I did not care about actually sending you the letters. I began to imagine that you were in front of me and I could talk to you. Perhaps I started to compose letters in my head right then, when the idea first crossed my mind. And in this way, I started to review everything again—your request for us to end things, and what I felt afterward, and what I had gone through beforehand—and I began to inscribe it all in my memory next to the medical terms and scientific names that I struggled for so long to memorize.

I trusted that this would benefit me somehow, but I did not know how.

The Day Before Your Request: How I Felt

Sadness does what it wants with us.

I was at the hospital, closing the door on a new body in the morgue. Fresh bodies had arrived ten minutes ago from the operating rooms. It was a depressing day. This was the first time in a while that we had received so many dead. I helped my fellow trainees, new and old. We took in the cadavers and began to put them in the refrigeration units. As usual, one of the trainees collapsed—it was his first day—and as usual I was surprised. I had never understood how someone could collapse in front of death. Since my university days, since the moment I killed and dissected my first frog, I had branded this collapsing

as something alien to me. This was confirmed later when we
entered the autopsy room for the first time during university
training. More than one student collapsed that day, and some
vomited, and others fled to the hall, and still others stood fast
but with anxiety plainly apparent on their faces. I would be
lying if I said that I was not anxious for a moment, but when
the doctor asked for a volunteer to step forward and take the
corpse's hand, I offered myself without hesitation. My anxiety
vanished in an instant, and I did as I was asked.

I recalled that scene as I slid the last corpse into cold
storage. Before I closed the door, I paused for several moments
and looked at the density of the darkness inside, at the black
aperture. For the first time since my university training, I felt
anxious, strange. Although I wasn't sure whether *anxious* and
strange were the right words to describe my feelings. Maybe what
I felt was closer to a sudden sadness. That which appears like

a wraith, coming quickly and going quickly, and leaves in its wake only incomprehension—for you never were accustomed to knowing, Sanaa, if you were happy or sad. Life would be so much easier if the absence of sadness meant happiness. But I know now that it's not like that. Standing before the refrigerator door, I felt absolutely nothing. Should I call this being numb? No. It's not numbness. I did care at that moment, and therefore I chose to call it, for the speed it possessed, a sudden sadness.

That night I was certain. I trusted my sadness. Something has happened, I said.

And I was right.

Choices

The next day I awoke beset by worries that would stay with me for a long time. Even now, as I write this sentence, I still carry some of them with me. Why do we choose? Why did I choose, for example, to love you? Why did you make the same choice to love me? Why did our two choices coincide? We could have made these choices but not dared to be candid with each other about them, and they would have remained only thoughts, with an equal potential for success or failure. When we choose, do we stop thinking? Who said that? Here I was, thinking that something had happened. Did something really happen, or is the truth of it that nothing happened at all, and I just thought it had, and then I based all of my choices on what was only an idea of mine? Isn't this possible?

What's in choices?

We humans choose because we think our choices might make us happier. We say *might* aloud, but internally we are longing for happiness. Inside we are sure that we made the right choices. Within we are certain, but publicly we hedge our words. We tell others about our choices scientifically, and we discuss the conflicting possible outcomes, each with its own unknown probability of occurring, that keep us from being certain. I find the whole thing strange and unjust. Why can't we enjoy that confidence in the correctness of our decisions in public, without resorting to such empty pretenses? Why don't we do this, when it would seem not extreme at all but natural for us? Wouldn't it relieve us of a great number of difficulties? Why must choices be hard, anyway, and defer to such an alarming quantity of factors, a complex web of possibilities?

That morning, as I was giving myself a headache with these concerns, I decided suddenly that all of this was pure sophistry, like you said to me once, Sanaa, the day you asked me to cease these endless speculations and to be more flexible and easy-going in how I dealt with things. You asked me not to squander my energy on what didn't deserve it, not to accumulate negative energy for no reason. These were the first of your observations. You hadn't said anything like this to me before. You even started to get upset as you were explaining your ideas, and I asked you, surprised, "What's going on?"

You rubbed your forehead and said, "Nothing . . . the university . . . I'm just a little tense."

I looked at you for a moment. Then I left you in the bedroom and went outside onto the terrace.

I don't know if you remember. I remember every detail of that moment—I thought about them for a whole week. The same week in which I found myself suddenly anxious in front of the corpse. All of this happened in seven days.

After getting out of bed, I picked up my cell phone and called you. Your phone was off, so I decided to go out. I got Rex to take him for a walk on Hamra Street. He barked in joy when I untied his leash from the post on the terrace. Did he believe he would see you? Perhaps. I had trained his barks. He was accustomed, whenever I untied his leash around this time of day and took him out for a walk, to meeting you.

Rex began to drag me behind him. He was more excited than I'd ever seen him. On the stairs, in the lobby of the building, on the sidewalk, and on the street, wherever Rex went I followed him without thinking. He raced on as I reined him in, trying to curb his speed. Then he stopped abruptly, turned toward me, and let out a strange sound, and when I looked around I found myself at the back entrance of Sanayeh Garden, where we had first met.

I called you again, but you didn't answer.

The Sadness of Time Reflected Upon Things

When we reached Hamra, Rex had begun to get tired. He started walking more slowly. His weariness suited my mood. After tying Rex to a telephone pole, I crossed the intersection by Jack & Jones and Vero Moda and sat on the steps of the Domtex building. A child passed by with his mother and was delighted to see the dog stretched out on the sidewalk. Rex woke up and raised his head so the boy could put his hand on it.

I left him with the child and his mother. I stared in their direction without seeing them. All three were transparent. My gaze traveled beyond them in the direction of the Piccadilly

Theatre and the clothing store beside it. The distances seemed to shrink, become shorter. It was not the first time that this had happened to me. You know, Sanaa, how I used to become lost in thought and cut out everything except that object upon which I wanted to focus.

I thought that we live among the reflections of time's sadness upon all things. The few glass façades on the stores dispersed around the intersection said this to me. The two intersecting streets said the same thing. The routes along which streams of cars flowed, exiting from the Piccadilly Theatre or passing by me on Hamra Street. The cats underneath the parked cars in the surrounding streets that I couldn't see but of whose presence I was certain. Even the dejected stray dogs of Beirut, two of whom I had come upon while walking Rex, and the faint light from the streetlamps at the beginning of evening, and the electrical wires that obscured any view of the sunset. To me all of these details bore witness to the reflections of time's sadness upon things. This time of mine. Yes, I said then in my mind, this time of mine, Sanaa, and suddenly I snapped to attention and came out of my reverie. My cell phone was ringing, and it was you who was calling. I came down from the stairs and stood on the sidewalk beside Rex.

The intersection became suddenly crowded, and a car stopped in front of me on the road. Its windows were tinted, hiding whoever was inside. I stared for several moments at my image reflected in the glass, and when the car moved on, I asked myself: Was there someone in the backseat of the car? Was he looking at me, although I could not see him?

The New Watch . . . the New Time

Life catches up with us wherever we are. At the peak of our "happiness," it caught up with us. I put the word in quotation marks because I still don't know whether we were truly blessed with happiness before the moment of our separation—which I try to, and cannot, identify—or not. I use *life* here in a new equation: for me, life became antithetical to all such clear things. Life as a whole, I mean. What I know is only that I was not sad, and maybe I was even enjoying myself at times, but does that mean we were happy?

I returned Rex to the terrace and went out again. I wanted to take a walk before our meeting. I headed over early toward the place we'd agreed on, walking slowly. I began to inspect the storefront windows again. I noticed that I was pausing only in front of windows where wristwatches were displayed. Maybe I like watches now? I thought. Had I, who had never bought a wristwatch, discovered my love for them on my way to see you?

I went in and bought a watch. I put it on my wrist, and I adjusted the time. I felt it ticking against my skin. After that, the time before our meeting began to pass slowly. I wandered in circles, thinking, for your voice on the phone had been different. You had answered my questions brusquely, your tone stripped bare of any emotion, so I had replied in the same way.

This was the first time I had noticed this difference. I began to trust my doubts and to prepare myself for that vague thing ahead. Did I know? Perhaps. Perhaps, but I tried not to think about it. I dismissed it from my mind. I followed your preferred advice and didn't burden myself with thoughts.

From Hamra I veered in the direction of the sea, then headed toward downtown. Your choice of place was odd, for the sidewalks that stretch from downtown to the St. Georges Hotel are devoid of pedestrians at this time of day, compared with our usual sidewalks in El Manara and Raouché. This increased my fear and the worries that I was trying to dispel. I could have taken a taxi, but I chose to walk. As I walked I began to look long and hard at my shoes. They were odd shoes, and I couldn't fathom why I had bought them. I understood all at once why you had always made fun of them. They truly were stupid. The sides curved slightly inward, and the heels were solid and thick, and the color had faded to the point where it elevated the shoes' original stupidity to a new level.

During my journey to you, I came upon a formation of ants marching quickly and in an orderly fashion across the pavement stones. I stopped and observed the movement of the caravan. The ants would not be distracted from their progress by anything. Even the intrusion of my shoe into the line they were following did not divert them from their course. The caravan simply altered its trajectory around my shoe with ease and continued heading toward the gap in the wall. I don't remember how long I stayed there watching the insects, but when I raised my arm and looked for the first time, really, at the new wristwatch, I found that the time of our meeting was approaching. I had confirmed that time, at least, did move.

And I thought: Maybe this discovery lightens the gravity of what I'm waiting for?

You Were One of the People with Answers

Do you know the people with answers? You were one of them, Sanaa. At least at the beginning. Who are the people with answers? They are those people whose faces don't ask any questions. You see them and they are serene. They suggest security. More than that. Their faces don't only disavow questions but are crowded with replies, and you know when you look at them that your questions are already resolved, that any action you take will not collide with an opposite reaction. Your relationships with these people are magic, like the magic of diving into a calm lake with no currents.

But this was before we had that meeting. This was before your promise to me of twenty-four hours. Did I use the verb *were* earlier? Let me see. Yes. Here: *You were one of them, Sanaa.* You were. Did I really know you? Did either of us know the other person?

I might keep going and ask: Does anyone in the world really know anyone else? If not, then why do some people reach a stage of boredom with each other? Why are they unable to find any topics at all to talk about? Why have all their stories vanished?

I used to look at your picture all the time on the home screen of my cell phone, or whenever it appeared either when I called you or when I received a call from a stranger of whom I had no pictures stored on the phone. It's a funny thing. Think of it this way.

You would appear on the screen in front of me at the following times:

1. When I closed the phone
2. As a permanent wallpaper behind the applications

3. When you called me

4. When someone called me whose number was not saved
   in the memory of the phone

On my phone, you had more than one personality and you possessed more than one meaning: closure, permanence, yourself, a stranger.

But what happened after that meeting? Were things no longer clear? Did your face no longer elucidate answers for me? Did you and the stranger become one and the same?

The Meeting: When You Didn't Explain to Me

When you got out of the taxi, you gave me a fleeting glance and then paid the driver and crossed the short distance between us, looking at the ground and fussing with something in your purse

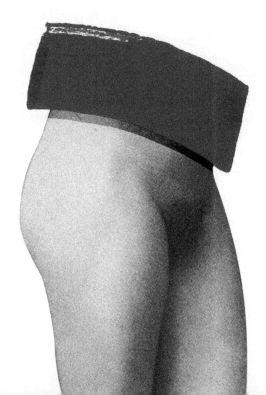

as you walked. This was the first time you had done this with me. I remained standing where I was and didn't come forward to meet you. You kissed my cheeks in a cursory way and said, "Hi," and then you started walking and I followed you.

The sidewalk is wide in this part of the city, and its paving stones are unusual, different from the ones that line the sidewalk in Raouché. Sand is scattered in the unfinished spots. Near here, the sea is paved over. Trucks pass this way many times during the course of the day. They keep going by until nearly nightfall, transporting sand and chunks of rock. The hotels project light from their upper floors toward the sky in early evening. More than one of the buildings contain stores that are always empty of customers. Cars race down the road, pulling up suddenly at the traffic lights.

All of this we saw as we walked together. Or anyway, I saw it. I don't know if you saw different things, but we were certainly not looking at each other. When we reached the St. Georges, the sidewalk disappeared. I walked on the edge of the road, and I grabbed your hand. My holding your hand in this way was strange, for even though we were sleeping together, neither of us had ever taken the other's hand, not when crossing the road, nor in the gesture of two teenage lovers. That was not us, I think.

We walked a little until we reached the broad sidewalk of the Corniche at Ain El Mreisseh. There you let go of my hand on the pretext that we had returned to the sidewalk. When you broke free of my captivity, I felt the sweat of the world on my palm, moist as it was from the sea spray. We kept walking without speaking, and my anxiety increased. It was possible that we would have remained like this until the end of our meeting if I hadn't decided to break the silence that had descended upon us.

"Coffee or hot chocolate?"

You shook your head, indicating neither one nor the other, and you said, "Nothing for me."

"Come on, I want something. What'll you have?"

You were silent for a moment, and then you asked, "Do they sell Smirnoff?"

When I crossed the road to get our drinks, you were watching me. I knew this, although you never told me so afterward. While I waited for the drinks, I observed you from afar as you turned your back and grasped the balustrade, and maybe you knew that I was doing this too, Sanaa.

I returned with the two cups and stood beside you. You fixed your attention on the sea and spoke without looking at me. I too looked straight ahead.

So it was that I missed much of what you said. Or maybe I wasn't listening. I was concentrating on the sea instead to get away from you. I remember only that you said you were going abroad for your doctorate and that you wanted to acclimate yourself to our separation before then, and that nothing between us had changed, it was just the circumstances, and that it was up to us, as mature adults, to try to avoid any emotional pressures that could undermine this maturity and the genuine experiences we'd had together.

You kept talking about how "genuine" what was between us had been, and then you asked if we could stay in touch, as friends. I realized at this point that the matter was settled, so I only smiled. Before we parted, as I was hailing a taxi for you, I asked, "Can I hug you?" You looked at me for a moment, and

across the short distance between us I was positive that I saw captive tears in your eyes.

Your choked voice when you answered confirmed their presence. "Of course."

We embraced for a few seconds, without laying our heads on each other's shoulders.

Me and Beirut in the Mirror

Usually when I get into a *service* taxi, I make sure to sit in the back and not to talk to the driver. This time I did the opposite. I greeted the driver and got into the front seat.

"Where to, *esteiz?*"

"To the university hospital. But take the Corniche the whole way, if it's no inconvenience."

"Gas is expensive, *esteiz.*"

"I'll pay you extra. Don't worry."

I waited for the driver to start talking to me. In Beirut, getting into the front seat of an empty *service* signals that the rider expects a certain conversational intimacy from the driver. Not much time passed before the driver began speaking, just as I had anticipated.

"Screw this country. No offense to you, sir, *esteiz.*"

As I had decided to talk to him, I agreed, "My God, yes, a thousand times over. You're right."

"What do you do for a living, *esteiz?*"

I stared into the side-view mirror as he spoke. "I'm a physician-in-training at the university hospital," I answered.

"God keep us from you. Ha ha," he said, and I laughed a little along with him. A moment later I watched him form in his mouth the largest spit wad I had ever seen in my life and then discharge it out the window to his left onto the road. For an instant I imagined that he was spitting on me, and for me, and I couldn't help but laugh. My laughter escalated, turning hysterical. As I was laughing, a disapproving expression fixed itself on the driver's face—probably he thought I was laughing at him. Yet this did not prevent him from asking me, "Are you okay, doctor? Is something funny?"

When I had taken possession of myself, I apologized to him and said, "Nothing . . . nothing . . . I just remembered something that happened to me once."

Then I fell silent. The driver continued along the Corniche, plainly still upset. Wanting to defuse the situation, I found myself continuing, "My fiancée just left me."

The driver looked at me and all traces of anger vanished from his face. They simply sank into his wrinkles. He started to say something, and then he hesitated. For my part, I began to watch the cars in the side-view mirror. I didn't know why I had admitted that to him. I expected him, like any other taxi driver, to start talking to me about you. To say that you "must have seen something" about our relationship that I hadn't. Or to curse you. These are predictable responses from a taxi driver. But this driver preferred, it seemed, not to embark on a discussion of personal matters or begin a conversation that could take an uncertain direction, or maybe he was just different from all other taxi drivers. I didn't know.

"I'll say it again. Screw this country, *esteiz*."

I nodded my head in agreement. The driver's hand reached into the pocket on the door next to him. He extracted an old cassette and fed it into the mouth of what remained of the car's stereo.

"A little music, doctor?"

Before I could answer him, the tape was screeching as though going into labor, and then I heard the voice of Ragheb Alama singing one of his older songs: *I want you near me, I want you, I'm seeking your consent, I'm seeking it.* Again I began to laugh, and this time the driver laughed with me.

"Laugh, doctor. What else is there in this world? Laugh . . ."

I continued laughing for another minute as the song played, and before Ragheb Alama had finished so that George Wassouf could start, the driver had launched into a speech about his children.

I let him tell his stories, nodding occasionally to show him I was listening, and went back to looking in the side-view mirror. Headlights gleamed in the glass, and I saw the sidewalks and buildings alternately walking, then running, behind us according to the density of the traffic and the speed of our car. I saw people hurrying by, and I heard songs playing from the cars stopped on my right.

In my solitude in the mirror, far from the stories of the driver's children and far from you, Sanaa, Beirut was more beautiful. I do not know how I was so certain of her abundant beauty in that instant, and I do not know if I was compensating for my lost love for you with a renewed love for the city, but I was confident that I was right, and that this city is beautiful, truly beautiful.

I am waiting to get in with a taxi driver one day who will greet me by saying, *Damn! How lovely Beirut is!* instead of *Screw this country!*

Who knows, Sanaa? Miracles happen sometimes.

The Beautiful Corpse

I dropped Rex off at Mama's for a couple of days. When
she asked me what was the matter, I said that I would be on
duty for several days in a row at the hospital in place of
a sick coworker, and then I rushed off down the stairs before
she could ask me about you. If she had, I would not have
been able to lie to her. My face would have exposed me, and
she would have sensed what I was feeling and not let me
go until I explained.

But I had not lied about the matter of having to stay at the
hospital. I found myself unable to return to my small apartment
after our separation, and my coworker's illness came along
at the right time to rescue me from this predicament and occupy
me with work. In this way, I imprisoned myself in the hospital
for four days, two consecutive shifts. It was the first time I had
worked two shifts back to back. I succeeded in escaping from
our agreement that we would talk again in twenty-four hours.
You, for your part, did not call.

I saw many bodies at the hospital. This time I was not anxious. I had regained my equilibrium. I was as enthusiastic
as if it were my first time. I autopsied two corpses on the first
night. The first corpse was an elderly man who was so emaci-
ated that his bones showed, and the second was a woman in her
twenties of sublime beauty.

When it came time to autopsy the woman, I couldn't help
staring at her naked body. I had never done this before. In my
work I was accustomed to never being aroused by the bodies I
saw. I don't know how I got it all mixed up. I don't know how I
found the body of the dead girl beautiful.

I left the room and went to wash my hands. I washed them more than once, and then I looked at the water flowing from the tap and after that at my face in the mirror. Sweat was dripping from my forehead, my eyes were sunken, my hair disheveled. Suddenly, almost without thinking about it, I put my head under the cold water. I kept it there for several moments.

I returned to the autopsy room and took up my work again without looking at the girl's face. I was seeing her as a collection of separate pieces now. I was carving her up with my eyes, and this helped me keep doing my job free from my previous thoughts.

After I finished, I went to the small break room to sleep. I found my colleague Ahmad sleeping on the other bed. I was overcome with weariness. I lay down gently on the bed. I felt a sense of deficiency. As though something had ended early, or maybe it lacked a conclusion. Or perhaps when it ended like this, it was as though it hadn't ended at all. With you, Sanaa, did I lose parts of myself? Did I leave things in you? So why do I not feel like you left in me anything worthy of mention? There is something here that is not complete. It all failed to satisfy me. I continued thinking about what I had lost until I felt the energy drain from my body through my limbs. I felt my impotence washing over me. Hardly a minute passed before sleep swept me away to other worlds.

The Replaying Dream

When do the replays start? And what happens then? Does boredom take over? Or do we experience it all again as though for the first time, as Warda promises us in one of her songs? Do we really mature by going back to the beginning?

For more than a month I've been dreaming the same dream. I see you, Sanaa, cut into pieces, like the beautiful corpse that I cut up with my eyes. Your head in one place. Your limbs in another. Your top section close by and your lower section further away. In the dream I rush to gather you up. I put you back together. I succeed at first, but then you slip from my hands in even smaller bits. My task becomes more difficult. I begin to collect the tiny pieces, and assembling you takes me longer this time. Then I do it. I step back to look at you, and I enjoy a single second with you while you are whole, and then before I can identify the meaning of the expression that sketches itself across your face, you break apart again, smaller, smaller, smaller, until the pieces of you become minute particles that I inhale, filling my airway. I awake coughing, my bed soaked in sweat.

I went to get Rex. Mama opened the door for me, and when she looked at me she asked me a strange question. "Why is your shirt hanging over your pants like that?"

This minor observation of hers made me realize that I had not worn a belt once since our breakup, nor had I fastened the collar of my shirt. I remembered everything in an instant: how I had laid aside the clothes that you had bought for me, and how I had lost the inclination to iron, and how the laundry was piling up in my apartment for the first time. Suddenly I had become one of those bachelors who pays no heed to the cleanliness of his rooms. But I understood that. I understood that I needed more than before to be comfortable, to wear loose clothes that were easy to put on directly out of the wash. And that I was searching for excuses to stay at the hospital, to help with anything at all however small, even if it was beneath me as a second-year trainee.

Each day I was avoiding suffocation. I was running away. But was I accomplishing anything at all by doing so?

The First Time

I returned in a hurry after my two work shifts so that I could bathe and then rush back with Rex to Mama's house. I stood under the shower enjoying the cold water. This was strange — I'm someone who can't stand washing in cold water even in the height of summer, so how could I stand to do it in April? The water began to make my whole body tingle. Whether this was due to my recent lack of sleep, or if cold water can have this effect on someone's body under any circumstances, I didn't know.

I found my penis growing erect under the shower. I was appalled by the idea that I could feel sexual desire when I was this exhausted. The scene started out comically, but presently it turned sentimental. I began to remember the first time we made love in my old apartment, and I smiled. At the time it had been funny. I was drunk and you were tipsy. I kept making sure that you really wanted to do it when we were drunk, and you kept assuring me that you were not drunk. "I'm just a little tipsy." We laughed. We laughed a lot. We didn't do much. The state we were in didn't allow us to. This was not the time for us to discover what we liked and what we did not. But it was the most radiant time in our story. Perhaps because it was the beginning? Perhaps. I don't know. I know that the details of the occasion are imprinted on my memory — how both of us smiled, for example, whenever one of us drew closer to the other, neither of us knowing what would happen. I could see my smile and your smile at the same time. I remember how we laughed when our first attempt didn't work out, and how we embraced, and slept, and how I awoke before you with the shy apparition of the sun. Even Rex was sleeping. I was alone, with the dawning of the morning and the filmy white curtain dancing in the draft from the partially open door. I did not stir then from the bed, Sanaa. I withdrew from you only slightly, just enough to grant me the sight of your body reclining close at hand. I counted your moles, the ones that stuck out and the ones that didn't, and I measured the distance between your shoulders with a glance, and I acquainted myself better with the color of your hair, which was changing beneath the shaft of sunlight entering through the balcony door, and I memorized the way you folded your legs as you slept on your side. And I won't lie: I looked at your butt. You know that. I will admit that to you soon, when you ask me, "Did you ever check out my ass?" And I will answer you, laughing, "Ho ho . . . more times than I can count." You will disapprove of this, and you will ask me how I can say this so very easily, and we will almost have an argument. So I will ask you, "Why are you asking me, then?" and you will reply, with some hesitation, "Any girl would wonder the same thing!"

How did the discussion end? I don't remember. But I remember how I came near you again in the bed that morning as you were sleeping and held you, and then suddenly, clinging to you, I found myself becoming erect again. Hardly a moment passed with you in my arms before you opened your eyes and looked at me to let me know that you could feel what was happening, and then you smacked me with the pillow and rose from the bed, saying, "Say good morning first!" I collapsed in laughter, and Rex seized the opportunity to start his morning round of barking.

I saw all of this while my eyes remained closed under the shower. When I opened them my sight was blurry, and the memory swelled before me in every drop of water that flowed down the tiles on the wall. Then I reached my hand to my penis and masturbated. The memories had ushered in the melodramatic phase of my bath. I began to cry. For the first time in a very long while I cried. I couldn't remember the last time I'd cried. I remember that I did not cry in front of you, not ever. My crying mingled with the water from the shower until I reached a point where I believed that I was not shedding tears, but that this water was pouring down on me from above.

How did we become two strangers like this, Sanaa?

The Slow Shattering

Sanaa. I resolved again and again not to think about you. My resolutions failed. There was much I still had to do before I could end the relationship. I wasn't yet capable of reconciling myself to the situation. A few days after the episode in the bathroom, I would look at photographs of us and conjure you afresh. The photographs brought me back to certain scenes, and then released me from these frozen moments to cast me into more distant visions. I started to remember how we would walk down the street—you preceding me, or me preceding you, or our four legs in step as we walked—and to count the times we had sat on a certain stone bench on the Corniche, or in the park, or on the street, and to recall how I used to watch you walk away when we parted in a public place or when a passing friend interrupted us and prevented us from continuing our conversation.

When I went to make tea in my small kitchen, I took out two mugs from habit, and then I realized what I had done and returned one of the two to the cupboard. I came back from the kitchen with a plate of pasta to the photographs that I'd spread out on the bed. I became aware, looking at a photo in which we sat side by side at a dining room table, that this time you would not insist that you were "not hungry" when I invited you to have some pasta too, and that you would not later steal a taste from my plate or allow yourself to be persuaded to get up and dish some for yourself. The photo between my hands had turned into a moment fixed in time. You are not here, I thought. You will not come in after a little while. Neither of us will observe from a distance how the other person looks in conversation, and neither of us will watch the other, engrossed in talking, to study how the muscles move in his or her face. We will not look at each other talking on the phone, or notice the crookedness of each other's teeth for the hundredth time, or realize the immaturity of each other's laughter, or stare at the pimples that appeared yesterday on each other's faces. From now on, I will not take note of how you swing your arms repeatedly in the same way when you walk, or how you try to level your shoulders when you are feigning confidence. Rex will not come over to you as you are stretched out on the sofa so you can rub his back and encourage him to climb into your lap to sleep. We will not go into stores together and pick out items to buy. From now on, we will not disagree, find ourselves having a stupid argument, and reach a compromise only because there are other people around.

There were too many things to summarize them all. It was too much to simply write off. Each of the photos spread out on the bed reminded me of my failure. I was not moving from one memory to another but from a failure to another failure.

The shattering was impossibly slow. It was not vengeance. It was pure masochism.

The Swing and the Pasta

Lying on the porch swing, I looked at the darkening sky and I started to swing. To the right. To the left. To the right. To the left. I heard the rattle of hinges, and then the sound of the front door closing. Rex stood up, barking, and headed toward the door of the terrace. I sat up straight in my swing, waiting for the intruder. I realized that the door had been locked. How had the intruder been able to open it, then? I remained waiting for several moments. A single idea gripped me, but I told myself I must be wrong. I heard Rex bark with excitement and make those sounds he makes when he greets someone familiar. Very little time passed before my expectations were proven true, and you appeared, Sanaa, holding the keys in your hand while Rex leapt up and down around you. You entered deliberately, walking slowly, and once you found me on the swing you stopped and smiled an unfamiliar smile.

I don't know how to describe my feelings at that moment. I won't lie and say that I was bursting with joy or that I felt hatred toward you in any clear way. Neither this nor that. I was lost. Stunned. I was falling. I was frozen in place, unable to speak. I looked at you. I examined you. Yes. Without meaning to, I was examining you. What had changed during this period of your absence? How much time had passed? Four months? A little more?

I continued to stare at you, speechless; perhaps I did not know what to say. You asked me if I wanted you to leave. I didn't answer. You nearly turned around and left, but I found myself, without meaning to, pronouncing your name.

We were, this time, two strangers in a way that was beautiful. For a moment, I at least delighted in our timidity. But soon I began to make comparisons. Our talk felt strained. We kept coming up with new topics of conversation only for them to die abruptly, and then we'd move right along to another topic of equal unimportance. Wanting to free us from this unease, I asked you, "You're going to stay in those clothes? You have more comfortable ones here; they're still in the closet inside."

You looked at me at first as though you were going to refuse. There was silence, and then you nodded hesitantly in agreement and went into the bedroom. A minute later I followed you, only to find that the door of the bedroom, contrary to our old custom, was closed. At that point, I decided to make some pasta. Food always helps to eliminate tension.

The Crack in the World

I woke at four a.m. I was naked in the bed. I turned over and you weren't there. The door to the terrace was open and the curtain swaying as usual. I got up slowly. I put on the pajama pants that were lying on the floor and went outside. I expected to find you standing there looking out at the city, but you were not there. I stopped for a few moments to look at the moon, watching the clouds as they passed across it, covering it, cleaving it in two.

Before you went, you had told me that you were leaving the country in two days. You said that you would take a tour of Europe before arriving at the university to begin your studies. You said that you had not been able to travel without seeing me first. I let you talk. You faltered at one point, and then you rushed on. You apologized for what we had just done. You said that it wouldn't change anything. I found myself saying, without knowing why, "And it didn't mean anything to you."

As I looked at the sky, I felt like everything was breaking apart. I saw the crack move across the world. Across objects. Split them into two halves. Expose their interiors. Bring forth from them new things that had been hidden. And presently the crack arrived at my heart. I began to cry again. But I was happy. In my story with you I had been lacking an ending, and I had gotten one at last.

Time Accelerated . . . Things Happened

It was as if time moved faster in your absence, Sanaa. As if I had entered a parallel world. The country exploded a week after your departure. When I heard the news, I was sure that it would turn into something big. Without doubt. This is a safety instinct that has been bred into our population. The awareness of danger. The levels of fear. When fear is practical and when we should be more nervous than afraid. Anyone who spent his childhood in this country knows these things. They are not suspicions. Maybe you're wrong, maybe all my worries are not just suspicions. You who returned to the country from the Gulf in the mid-nineties. Hadn't I felt like something had happened between us even before you told me you wanted to end things? This was it. The very thing.

I didn't go to the hospital right away. I wanted to give my worries a chance. Although who knew—you might get the better of me this time and be right. I sat on the sofa in front of the TV watching the stilted press conferences. Suddenly I heard the sound of shots outside. I hurried onto the terrace and looked down. A man was standing in the street, brandishing a gun. He fired several bullets into the air. Then he stopped and began to shout. Only his curses were intelligible: "You sons of whores . . . you sons of whores!"

I went back inside and looked at the TV. The ticker at the bottom of the screen was packed with news. When had this all happened? I got out my small overnight bag, put some clothes into it, and left in a hurry for the hospital.

The Dead Corpses . . . the Undead Corpses

Our hospital was overflowing with the wounded, and as the events went on, the officials mobilized and began to redistribute duties. We started to accept the dead corpses as they were, without documents. Other doctors had their hands full over-seeing the emergency cases.

Dead corpses. I stopped for a moment, pondering this phrase. Are there any corpses that are not dead? Yes. I have a theory about this. There are corpses that are not dead. Corpses that do not make you feel like you could turn them into stories are dead corpses. Humans differ even in their deaths. There are among them those whose light is dim, and there are those who shine even once their souls are gone.

How many corpses arrived on the first day? There were not that many. They were distributed among several hospitals in the area. But a single one of these corpses was worth a thousand other corpses. The corpse that arrives with a bullet hole in it or after an unexpected accident is different from the corpse of someone who died from a heart attack or during an operation or even from cancer. In cancer cases — though I haven't seen many of these firsthand — the body reaches its end gaunt and tired, with a color that lacks color. The corpse that comes to you after an operation is stitched up, yes. Disfigured, but it has been expertly put back together, and its arrival might be antici-pated given how many patients die during operations. As for the corpse that arrives at the hospital dead after an act of violence, it is different. It hasn't only come before its appointed time like the rest of these dead. It has come before its appointed time, and it has come with a story. It has come as an exception. Per-haps the difference is that its arrival is unexpected, and therefore exceptional? At least in the present year. I do not know. I do not know if my logic is correct and my theory convincing. It's not important. Perceiving things and understanding them is an entirely personal matter. Thus I see, thus I believe, and thus am I certain. I do not know how the situation would have been during the civil war. Would the corpse riddled with bullets have disengaged itself from exceptionalism? Would it have lost its story on account of its unexceptionalism?

I was tired. Not because of the work. The prevailing atmosphere itself was tiring. The televisions were on in the corridors and the waiting areas and the patients' rooms, and some of the staff were lingering to watch even though this was against the rules. Is an abundance of exceptionalism tiring? Perhaps. This outbreak of events, disrupting the accustomed rhythm, becomes tiring as the events drag on, especially if you are waiting for them to end and haven't conceded yet that it is they that have become unexceptional, routine.

The second day, I had two corpses to deal with. They told me that these were two brothers, and that their story was one that the people of Beirut would be talking about for days. I would read it in the newspapers a week later in greater detail. In summary, the first brother was wounded by a bullet. His brother picked him up, carried him to the car, and rushed to the hospital. Militants stopped him at a roadblock, and when they found the injured man with him, they let him pass. Hardly had the car gone through when bullets rained down on it. The second brother was killed and joined the first. The two corpses were not put in the same room. But I could not help returning to the face of the first brother when I saw the face of the second. They were two corpses that were similar to the point of being identical. This is a story. These two corpses have not yet died.

But I did not know, Sanaa, that all of this was nothing worthy of mention beside the story that I would find myself a part of.

Sometimes I wonder: Would I have been a covert witness to this story had you still been in my life? Something says to me that your exit from it allowed other elements to appear.

Maybe life was sweeping over me, now that it had smashed our bubble in which I had imprisoned myself for years? *Maybe*, I say, for this is all too much to be convincing. But again, must our personal stories be convincing?

Half-Faced Drawings

After three days at the hospital, I returned home. I walked down empty streets, avoiding the armed men who appeared from time to time on Hamra Street. Things had stabilized somewhat despite the militarized appearance of the street. I arrived at my apartment at six p.m. without significant problems. Rex gave me an enthusiastic welcome. He had not seen me in three days, and his food had almost run out. After washing out his special food and water dishes, I refilled them. Rex busied himself with his fresh meal, and I went in to bathe. In the bathroom mirror, I didn't know myself. My eyelids were drooping, my eyes surrounded by black halos for the first time. Even during my time at the university this hadn't happened to me. I bathed quickly, and then I threw myself onto the bed and fell asleep faster than I expected. I don't remember my dreams, but I remember a vision of a field drowned in water, and my feeling of suffocation. I wouldn't have woken up had Rex not licked my face. I sat up in bed and looked at the clock. It was just after five a.m. How I had slept those nine hours, I didn't understand. The dog jumped down, stood in front of the apartment door, and began to bark, begging me to take him out. The three days he hadn't gone outside had put me in this predicament: I had no choice but to walk him at dawn.

The streets were empty, devoid of any trace of life. I walked up and down with Rex. He ran in front of me. He would stop and then bark at me to hurry up. When I was tired of chasing him, I went over to him and he began to lick my hand. I caught him by surprise and grabbed his leash. He made a sad sound, but then he gave in and modified his pace to match the speed of my steps.

Although I kept my grip on him, I let him direct me. I found him leading me out of a side street onto the main avenue of Hamra Street. There, a young man was cleaning the wall. I didn't grasp what was happening at first, but after a few moments of watching him from afar I understood that he was preparing the wall so he could paint on it. I approached him, tying Rex to a nearby telephone pole. The young man was struggling to stick pieces of paper to the wall, so I decided, with barely a thought, to help him.

I helped him mount the sheets of stiff paper. We did not talk. We exchanged glances and we both smiled, and he gave a nod of thanks. As I fixed the papers in place, the young man busied himself removing paints and other equipment from his bag and placing them on the ground. Then he began to spray. A few minutes after he stopped, we took down the papers one after another. The picture began to become clear: a repeating

pattern of the top halves of different faces arranged close together in a horizontal line.

The young man was preparing to stow his implements when I saw an armed man emerge from a side street. He looked in our direction and then began to approach us. And just as I had not understood why I had stopped to help the young man, I did not understand why I untied Rex in a hurry from the telephone pole and took off running. I didn't look behind me, and I didn't hear the man with the gun call out to me.

I remembered you as I ran, Sanaa. I remembered the way you move. The way you run. How you use your hands when you want to prove a point. I kept my thoughts on you. I was waiting for a bullet in my back, and I felt myself beginning to sweat, but the bullet did not come.

Instead, the opposite happened.

I Saw Death for the First Time

I took refuge in the lobby of a building and stopped to catch my breath. Hardly had I begun to go back outside when a car sped suddenly by on the street. I retreated quickly. Rex was completely silent, as though he sensed the gravity of the situation. I remained standing there for several minutes, listening carefully. The street was calm, with no sounds I could detect. With some hesitation, I decided to go out. I tied Rex's leash to my wrist and emerged slowly. There was no one there, and it had begun to rain. I looked down Hamra Street in the direction I had come from, and I could not see anything moving. I decided to return Rex to the house and then head to the hospital. I continued walking quickly till I reached the end of the street. I told myself that I would turn onto the first side street on the right that I came upon and return to my apartment from there, and after that I would go to the hospital. I was jogging and so was Rex, who was still quiet. I reached the first street. I stopped at the corner to catch my breath. Then I looked back once more. Before I continued on my way, I turned to face forward again. There was something heaped in the middle of the street. I stood still for a moment, not knowing what to do. Should I approach or continue my escape?

When I had made sure that no one was around, I approached the thing I had seen, and my suspicion proved correct. It was the same man with the gun, lying on the ground awash in blood. Rex tried to get closer to the blood, but I commanded him to back off with a word that he understood. I bent over the man and pressed my fingers to his neck, contaminating my hand with his blood until the rain could return to wash it off.

There was no pulse. I stepped back, not knowing what to do. This was the first time I had confronted death fresh, not as a corpse. I was not thinking like a doctor. I was not thinking of what I had to do to restore the man's pulse. It horrified me, the condition he was in. This man who had been aiming his weapon at me just minutes ago was now drowning in his own blood. I turned around again. I could not see the wall where the drawing was, nor the young man who had been there. The street curved and that part of it was out of sight. I turned around again to look at the other end of the street. It was empty. No cars, no people on the balconies. Nothing.

I moved at once. I grabbed Rex by the leash—luckily he obeyed me—and raced back to the side street that I had intended to go down earlier.

I thought that I should use my cell phone to call the hospital, but I was struck with anxiety. I was nearly home now. I found a public telephone, and fortunately I had a calling card with me. I called from there.

I was anxious, exactly like my classmates from my university days whom I used to mock.

A Witness to Other Lives

I was waiting in the ER for the arrival of the gurney from the ambulance. I had returned here quickly after dropping off Rex at the apartment and changing my clothes. I remained in the ER on the pretense of helping some colleagues with administrative matters. I was trying to enter the contents of the paper folders in front of me into the computer system, but to no avail. Despite the simplicity of the task, my mind was elsewhere. I thought about the man. Had he really been dead, or not? No. No. There had been no pulse. He was dead. Surely, he was dead. I left my work and went to stand against the wall beside the elevators. From here they would bring him in, if they brought him. From here. I thought of you, Sanaa. I thought that these things would not have happened if we were together. I would not have been on duty at the hospital like that, and I would not have returned to the house yesterday, and I would not have fallen asleep, and perhaps I would not have dreamed, and Rex would not have awoken me insisting that I take him for a walk. At the very least, you used to be the one who walked Rex, and I used to spend my free time with you and not at work.

Now I had lost my safe harbor. Now I knew the meaning of safety. Now I understood how stupid my idea was that safety only led to boredom.

I thought about all of this as I looked down at the shoes I despised, and I decided then and there that I would buy new shoes as soon as I could leave and the stores opened for the day.

I looked up, preparing to go back and carry on with my work, and I saw a pregnant woman in front of the elevator clutching her stomach, her pain evident. I wanted to go to her and find out what was wrong, but just at that moment the double doors of the emergency room opened and the gurney entered. On it was the man whose injuries I had reported. The gurney passed rapidly between me and the pregnant woman. Following the man with my eyes as he moved away, I saw a strange thing on his arm that I hadn't noticed in the street: a telephone number and address were tattooed there.

Hardly had the gurney passed when the woman began to scream. I went to her and gripped her hand, and several nurses hurried toward us to help her. She was giving birth.

Wasn't it as if I were being targeted by strangers that day, Sanaa? From the young man drawing, to the militiaman, to the pregnant woman in the ER? How did I become suddenly a witness to the lives of all these people? How did I intrude on their lives, and how did they intrude on mine? How did I get in like this, and how did I become a part of stories I do not understand? And would I be able, if my intrusion was meant for a purpose, to play my role?

The Corpse That Might Not Die

I stood in the autopsy room. Other doctors had come with me. After figuring out the man's name, they had called his family. His neighbors arrived and identified him. They said that he lived with his sick mother. Militiamen have sick mothers, Sanaa? Other men came too, wearing clothes similar to his, and looked at him and nodded their heads. Were these his companions? Had they left their weapons outside the hospital?

I stood by silently. I helped take the corpse out of the refrigerator and put it back in. I did not help to wash it. I only became acquainted with his face after they washed it. I had not registered what his face looked like when he was lying in a heap in the middle of the street. It had been obscured with blood. I was the only one who knew him, Sanaa, among all those who came and cast their eyes on him. This is what I thought as I stood before his corpse. This corpse, I alone knew. This corpse, I alone knew its final scene, not his mother, not his neighbors, not the other militiamen who were his companions. Would he have killed me if I had kept standing there and not fled? Had he been aiming his weapon at my back before the car struck him? Where is the young man who was drawing? Does he know me like I know him? Wasn't he there too? Was he killed? Is he still alive? Who killed this man now before me? And did anyone see me as I bent over him? Had he been alive?

The questions continued to assail me whenever I stepped away from my work for a few minutes to pace the corridors of the hospital. Every time I took out the corpse, I saw the telephone number and address tattooed on the man's arm. You know me. I never remember numbers, Sanaa. I couldn't even memorize your phone number. I rely on my cell phone to save them for me. You know that, and we quarreled over it once. But here it was different. I found myself memorizing the number on his arm without intending to. Whenever I took

out the corpse so someone could see it, I said the number
silently to myself before I confirmed what it was by looking.

I was before an undead corpse, bearing a story some
part of which I knew.

I was before a corpse that might not die. With me it will
not die.

The Children's Ward

They took him away on the following day. I don't know what
happened to him after that, and I did not make an effort to find
out from my colleagues at the hospital. On my breaks at work,
I would sit by myself in the hospital café, take out my small
notebook, and begin to write down over and over the number
I had learned by heart. Was I afraid to lose it? Didn't I need
to lose it? To let this corpse die? I didn't know what I was doing.
I recorded the number between the lines of what I wrote to
you. I repeated it in the margins of the pages. It was always
there, a riddle clearing the way for the story to end.

The number distracted me from you. For the first time in
a while I was not thinking about you. Had I needed to witness
death in front of me before I could bring our story to an end?
I was only seeking a safe way out. Was this it? I don't know.
I don't know, but I don't believe so. I spent the next day at the
hospital although it was my day off. I walked around with
headphones in my ears. My footsteps kept time with the music.
I saw elderly patients wandering the corridors, escorted by IV
drips. Some of them laughed at me, and some of them pointed,
and the rest continued on their way and did not pay me any
attention. I noticed during these walks of mine how hospitals

vary from one part to another. Between the morgue and the rooms for patients there is a big difference. There we forfeit hope, and here we cultivate it. This observation may be obvious, but I only became aware of it then. As I removed the headphones from my ears, I remembered the pregnant woman who had squeezed my wrist as she went into labor, before they took her away. I went down to the ER and asked about her and how her delivery had gone.

I took the route to the children's ward for the first time. Inside, babies cried loudly. A female doctor who was a colleague of mine came up to me and asked me what I was doing there. I told her that I wanted to check on the child of the pregnant woman from the ER and to see for myself that he was in good health. She led me outside, and from behind the glass partition she pointed out the boy and told me that he was fine. They would take him to his mother shortly so she could nurse him.

I asked if I could accompany her to check on the health of the mother as well. She looked at me, puzzled, but she didn't ask me to explain. I went to sit on a chair in the hall and wait for her.

The Decisive Moment

Has our story really never been told before, Sanaa? Is it an exceptional love story, or a common one? Does our story resemble the stories of others, with only minor differences? Have they wound up with similar endings, or did they do better than us? I thought about all of this as I reread the pages I had written to you, and I came to the decision that I would not send them. The letters that had started out addressed to you turned along

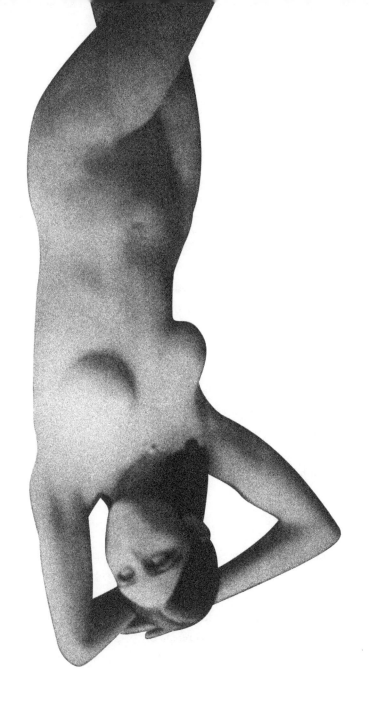

the way into scribbled diary entries, which I then typed up and organized on the computer. My intention behind writing them had been to understand: When was the moment after which everything between us changed?

And now I understood.

There was no single decisive moment at all.

We had always lacked good communication. I was comfortable in the relationship. Comfortable because I did not have to explain, because we did not go into detail. I convinced myself that this relationship was a mature relationship, but I was wrong. When did I realize this? When I saw the woman holding her child in her hospital room. When did I realize this? When her young husband entered the room suddenly and they both began to cry, and when he began to apologize to her, while she told him not to apologize, and when he held his child, and when . . .

I realized that I had been searching in the wrong place, and that I was the one to blame for our relationship's failure. I, who would use flimsy excuses to distance myself from you when you tried to get closer to me. I, who, when I saw that you were tired or sad, would ask you what was wrong, and when you denied that there was anything the matter, I would not ask again.

Even when I slept with you for the last time, something was missing. I did not ask you a single question as we made love. I did not stop once to check with you before taking another step. You let me in the whole time without saying anything. It was my last chance and I wasted it.

I had always been like this and I did not realize it . . . until today.

I wanted to call you. With some insistence, I got one of your friends to give me your number, but I changed my mind as I was dialing the final digit. I did not want to hurt you even more. For you have moved on with your life, and I must do likewise. Were we destined to meet again someday, and indeed this may happen, I would try hard to apologize to you without explaining too much.

I believe that you would understand, and that you would understand that I understood this, and perhaps you would smile.

Who knows?

Do I Let the Corpse Die?

In the deluge of events, I forgot my previous promise to myself. A week after the incident in the emergency room, I will look at my stupid shoes and be reminded of it. I will get up to put them on, as I do every morning, and I will be surprised to find a hole in one of their soles. How did I not notice this hole growing, even though I wore the shoes practically every day? And how does a hole appear in the sole of a shoe overnight?

I will throw away the shoes and put on another pair that I hardly ever use, and I will go out to Hamra Street determined to buy new ones. You don't know, Sanaa! They may be less stupid this time than their predecessors! I will walk down the sidewalk in the opposite direction of the traffic. And I will find that life has returned to normal, and that some of the store owners are beginning to patch the bullet holes in their shops and to replace the shattered glass façades. I will stand for a few moments in front of the graffiti, and then I will continue on my way. The street will be crowded just as before, and the cleaning crews working in their usual fashion. I will stop to buy a newspaper from a kiosk so that I can follow what's happening. I will cross the Vero Moda–Jack & Jones intersection, and there I will stop, looking at the contents in the window of a shoe store. I will select a pair by sight, and then I will go inside.

As I wait for the clerk to bring me shoes in my size, the young artist, the same one I saw that night, will enter, fine and unhurt, talking on the phone with a friend of his, or rather a lover. This I will understand from his manner of speaking and his choice of words (I hear him say *baby* and utter the name of a man). He will not see me at first, because he will be absorbed in examining the shoes as he talks on the phone. Then he will conclude his call and put his phone away in the pouch he is carrying. He will select a pair of shoes on display, check its size, and then turn toward me.

We will look at each other for a moment, and then he will pause and sit down on the bench opposite, confused.

The store clerk will come back with my size and ask the young man if he needs help, and still confused, he will request his size in the pair he is holding.

After the clerk returns to the rear of the store, I will look at the young man again, smile, and ask him, "Are you okay?"

"I'm okay."

As he nods at me in answer, I will remember the telephone number with which I filled the margins of my journal entries. I will remember the numerals in sequence, digit by digit. As I walk in my new shoes, returning to my apartment, I will come to the conviction that this encounter was no coincidence. This encounter has shown me a new path. Perhaps I should call the number as soon as I reach the apartment. Perhaps I must let the man's corpse die so that I can move on with my life. Perhaps I must bury the death that I witnessed; perhaps I must help, as much as possible, to bring the story of which I was a part to a close.

Perhaps.

Author Thanks

DEEPEST THANKS to everyone who helped me, directly or indirectly, in bringing this work into being.

Thank you to Mohammad Rabie, who read the novel before anyone else, and to Zeina G. Halabi for suggesting certain revisions and for her encouragement throughout, and to the ever-supportive Sanaa Khoury, and to Leila Arman, whose Twitter feed provided essential details for the novel's final chapter.

Thanks are necessary as well to Mohamed Gaber, Fadi Adleh, and Barrack Rima, the visual authors of this novel, and to Jana Traboulsi, without whose tireless artistic drive this work would not have appeared as it is today, and to the Arab Fund for Arts and Culture (AFAC), whose grant made the project possible.

A final thanks to the unknown readers on Facebook, Twitter, Tumblr, WordPress, and Goodreads for always encouraging me to keep writing.